D0713068

The New Savages

ALSO BY TIMERI MURARI

The Marriage

The New Savages

TIMERI MURARI

M

SBN 333 18444 0

First published 1975 by
MACMILLAN LONDON LIMITED
London and Basingstoke
Associated companies in New York
Dublin Melbourne Johannesburg and Delhi

Produced by computer-controlled phototypesetting,
using OCR input techniques, and printed offset by
UNWIN BROTHERS LIMITED
The Gresham Press, Old Woking, Surrey

To my mother
JOGI
in memory

The unfit and the unneeded! The miserable and despised and forgotten dying in the social shambles. The progeny of prostitution—of the prostitution of men and women and children, of flesh and blood, and sparkle and spirit; in brief, the prostitution of labour. If this is the best that civilisation can do for the human then give us howling and naked savagery. Far better to be a people of the wilderness and desert, of the cave and the squattingplace, than to be a people of the machine and the Abyss.

–Jack London

1

MARKO awoke and felt good. Instinctively he knew why. It was Friday morning. He lay in the large bed, which completely filled the small, bare room, fifteen minutes longer before jumping out. His everyday clothes lay where they had been thrown on the chair. Creased brown trousers, a creased shirt and a worn green cardigan. The right heel of his black platform shoes, which he'd only had two weeks, was coming apart. Cheap stuff he'd bought for six sheets, which he promised himself to return and demand his money back.

Thrown on a dismantled cycle in the hall were his overalls and pixie woollen cap. He scooped them up as he passed. He went straight to the record-player in the front-room, dropped an Isaac Hayes on to the turntable, turned up the volume and left the room. His aunt looked resigned. Ivor always had to have his music, morning, noon and night. Never softly either. She poured him a mug of tea and dropped four marshmallow biscuits on to a saucer. She was an old Irish woman in her seventies. She could have been younger, but age hadn't been gentle with her. It had blasted and ravaged her body and face into two shapeless, crumpled masses. Her body, heavy and bloated, was hidden by a grubby nylon blouse and a faded grey skirt; her face seemed to have no bones for the mantle of loose flesh, and her once-blue eyes were a rheumy grey. She moved to the window and looked up at the sky as Marko returned.

'I think it's going to be a nice day, Ivor,' she said. 'Bit warm though, I feel. Hot.'

Marko didn't glance out; his aunt always talked weather.

'True,' he said. He always said 'true' when he didn't want to talk much.

Apart from the sky, all that they could see of Liverpool through their top-floor window was tenements like theirs. Row upon row of tenements, new and old, three-storey, six-storey, ten-storey, all shaken out of the same mould, separated haphazardly by narrow streets and rectangular concrete playing-areas. Their own tenement, Duff Gardens, stood low down on the concrete and asphalt banks of the Mersey, only a few blocks up from the Coburg Dock, and the steep slope hid the rest of the city from view . . .

Buried beneath eight centuries of mud and gravel and sand and brick is a liver-coloured swamp. Liverpool is the concrete and asphalt tombstone for that swamp. They haven't completed it as yet. Each day they put down another layer of concrete, another layer of asphalt. The concrete rises upwards in the shape of stark, severe tenement blocks; the asphalt flows outwards like a slow-moving river of lava to cover the earth with a black encrustation. There are spirits down there in that swamp, groaning sleepless under the enormous weight of this tombstone. They are the poor. Crones, hags, serfs, peasants, seafarers, slaves, dockers, the starving, the sick, an endless march of poor. They rise up at night, slipping through the still-uncovered cracks and fissures in the earth, heavy with curses, their skinny frames shackled to their pain and misery. Drifting in with the mists from the Mersey, invisible, odourless, they come to haunt the rich who fattened off them. Liverpool was the rich red artery of an empire, and it was the rich who in the sixteenth and seventeenth centuries earned £300,000 a year from the slave trade, more still when half the country's exports moved down the Mersey in the eighteenth century and a fortune when one-seventh of the world's shipping used the port in the nineteenth century. The poor carried all this wealth up the sloping banks of the Mersey to those elegant houses on top of the hill, and that was the only time it touched their lives. In 1794 one-fortieth of the city lived in poorhouses. In 1832 Liverpool boasted of the largest poorhouse in the nation. In 1847 the Irish escaping the potato famine swelled the numbers of poor. In 1943 one-third of the houses were unfit for human habitation. In the 1970s the poor have inherited Liverpool. In the last ten years the population has dropped from one million to 600,000. The rich and the middle class have fled to the suburbs, the picturesque villages, the country estates. Each night the spirits come to haunt and find only their descendants, the poor . . .

Marko stood in front of the mirror above the fireplace. He picked up the very long-toothed, narrow comb and began carefully straightening out his Afro. The hair surrounded his delicate face with an eight-inch-deep black halo which made him look older than seventeen. On the television set is a photograph taken the year before with his hair short. His clenched right fist is raised high above his head, straight and stiff and proud. He looks a fierce child awaiting its own destruction. There are two other photographs; in both his face is the lone black one in the school football team.

His aunt was still ruminating about the weather. At times it would be too warm, at others too cold. They'd lived together fifteen years and he'd taken her name–Markham–as his. She couldn't remember when she'd left Ireland. As a young girl, she'd say, and never been back.

He finished patting his hair into shape and sat down to breakfast. He ate two of the biscuits and slipped the other two into his pocket for lunch. He never ate much. Once he had tried to go without food for two days and it had weakened him. He was a slim, wiry boy and could have done with eating more often. He finished his tea and returned to the bedroom while his aunt cleared the table. He sat on the bed and pulled out a packet of Rizla skins. He licked three of the fine cigarette papers and stuck them together; two lengthwise and one across. He broke a cigarette and spread the loose tobacco evenly over the papers, searched his pockets and found the screw of silver paper. He opened it carefully and removed the small, brown fragment of drag. The silver paper was reshaped into a tiny spoon, the drag dropped in the hollow and warmed gently by a match. Marko crumbled the drag, sprinkled it over the tobacco, rolled it carefully and licked the joint closed. He lifted the hair over his right ear and stuck the joint behind it. The hair completely hid it. He shoved three matches into his hairline above his forehead, the fourth he chewed on.

'What time'll you be up?' his aunt asked as he pulled on his overalls in the hall.

' 'Bout two,' Marko said. Every Friday, he returned to the flat at the same time. 'Later, Daisy.'

' 'Bye.'

Marko stepped out of the flat onto the long balcony that ran the whole length of the building. From where he stood he could see parts of the Mersey. It was flat and empty. On the opposite bank, Birkenhead was a dense scramble of docks, warehouses and tenements. The rest of his view was hidden by the blocks of Duff Gardens. Directly opposite a young white woman was hanging out her washing, while down below workmen were laying paving-stones over a small patch of bare earth and three Boot Boys were kicking a ball around.

Marko's head began to hurt. This had happened every day for as long as he could remember. His head and the nape of his neck felt as if they were being squeezed slowly and steadily. The pain grew worse as he ran down the six flights of stairs. It would stay with him all the way until he had covered the mile to safety and Windsor Street. Marko was unfortunate. He was a black kid living in Boot Boy territory, where every wall was painted with the names of his enemies. (Each year their titles changed. Skinhead, Boot Boy. . . .) Tony and Tommy, Steve and Bill, Dick and Chas and Bicklo. BICKLO was on nearly every wall. The King Boot Boy painted his name on walls throughout his territory as a reminder of his power.

High above the scribble of names everywhere was a single stark word–WHACKER. It was always in black, and isolated from the others, as if it belonged to someone very special and very different. Graffiti in the tenements are never erudite. 'Bicklo is ace' is the only complete sentence to be found among them. The kids have no clever messages, no profound insights into life. They possess only their names and these they paint up, over and over again, granting themselves a brief immortality.

Marko crossed Grafton Street. It was long and narrow and ran parallel to the docks–Toxteth, Brunswick, Coburg, Queen's, King's, Wapping. Going south it reached into the Dingle, and north into the city centre. Marko walked with his fists clenched in the pouch of his overalls and his eyes constantly flicking over every person that moved. He wished at times he could see round corners. He was a creature of habit. Each day he followed the same zigzagging route up to the black ghetto. It was a long climb through tenement country, along narrow, scantily surfaced cobbled streets, across concrete playgrounds and tiny patches of waste ground. Scattered along his route were a few shops–grocers, newsagents, launderette–and pubs.

He reached Beaufort Street, and hesitated at the corner. Six months ago, a gang of Boot Boys had been waiting at that corner. Marko had steeled himself and passed through their ranks. When he was ten yards up Brassey Street, he looked back. They were following. He hadn't lingered. He scorched up Brassey Street, across a patch of waste and into Upper Stanhope Street. The Boot Boys had lost him on the waste: Marko was too fast for them. They never needed to run as fast as he had to. They had no pigs or Boot Boys to give them running practice and that made them flat and slow. Marko's head was splitting. There were two Boot Boys sitting

4

on the steps of a tenement. Silently they watched him pass. He refused to look back. Last winter he'd been passing that same block with his sandwiches tucked into his pouch. A boy was walking towards him. When they were two feet apart, the boy suddenly launched a kick at Marko's belly. Marko knew it was coming a split second before the boot lifted. His mind was trained to sense the sudden pump of adrenalin in another man's body, to read the signals of violence a second before they surfaced. He jumped back with both feet and the boot caught him in the sandwiches. Marko sidestepped and put his boot into the boy's thigh. Before he could kick again the fight was over. The boy dodged and ran. Marko had taken out the sandwiches and kissed them. If he had gone down, the boy would have ripped his head off. Over the last six months, however, the Boot Boys hadn't pressured him too much. He'd sent word that if anyone battered him he'd come back even if it took the rest of his life and batter the shite out of the boys who'd done it. They knew Marko never joked.

He crossed St James's Place. It was piling up with morning traffic, and Marko dodged the cars. Halfway up Dexter Street, he involuntarily glanced up to the second floor of a tenement on the right. His mother lived there with a honky and his children. Marko decided not to take a chance that she might see him and cut back through to Upper Stanhope Street. Marko wasn't afraid of his mother. He just didn't feel like confronting her this morning.

His headache, which had begun to ease as he was now near Windsor Street, increased as he remembered he had to pick up some tools from James Place, a three-sided tenement that faced the old cathedral.

The Anglican cathedral soars above the surrounding tenements like a fortress over squalid villages. Dipping down behind it into a deep moat is a beautiful green park protected by iron railings. They call it the 'old' cathedral and those huge, black, rain-stained sides make it look medieval, though they only began building at the turn of the century and still haven't completed it. The same family of craftsmen have been labouring on it for fifty years. The tall crane hovers permanently in line with the cathedral tower, which is flat and stubby and resembles the crowns of those ancient English kings.

From the tower you have a clear view of Liverpool. The cathedral faces the Mersey and those empty wharves stretching along the banks as far as the eye can see. The countless jetties cut into the water like a square-toothed saw. To the north and west, the city dips and rises, with here and there the spikes of smaller churches, the tower of the new Roman Catholic cathedral, the tower restaurant in the city centre and the high-rise apartment-building on Dove Street. There are occasional patches of green to the south–Sefton Park and Princes Park.

Marko never looked at the cathedral. He studied James Place carefully and warily moved to the entrance.

Trenchy, in the ground-floor flat to the left of the entrance, watched Marko through the window. Peter Trench should have been in school. His mother had woken him up before leaving for her work as a cleaner in the Town Hall. Trenchy, however, always dawdled. He hated this last year in school. Trenchy was a slim, handsome boy of sixteen with a broad face and a slight turned-up nose. He was always neatly dressed. With his shoulder-length auburn hair, and blazer, he could pass for a grammar-school boy. He used schoolboy slang rather than obscenities and at times acted far older than his age.

It was 9.10 and school had started at nine. Trenchy didn't hurry; St Martin's was only a five-minute walk away. Marko passed through the archway entrance and Trenchy crossed the flat to the front window. It looked out on the asphalt courtyard. There were a few children, both black and white, playing. They looked at Marko curiously; most of them knew who he was. 'That's Marko,' one said, though not aloud. Marko didn't allow any honky to call him that. Within his hearing, they had to say Ivor.

Marko ran up two flights and along the balcony to Number 42. Nearly every brick he passed was scrawled with the word BICKLO. Where it could be written it was written. As the word multiplied so Marko's headache increased. The intensity of being watchful and alert was beginning to tire him. He was now in the heart of Bicklo's territory.

Trenchy watched Marko all the way. In some ways he respected Marko. Marko was the only nigger who'd ever caught him. Trenchy prided himself on being a very fast runner, which was why he'd never been caught. Until one evening he turned a corner and there was Marko. Trenchy turned and ran. Marko had scorched after him. Trenchy was wearing new platform shoes and couldn't run at top speed. Marko caught him and swung two punches before Trenchy broke and escaped.

Marko collected the brushes and a scraper from the flat and

asked the woman if anything else needed to be done. He had enjoyed working for her because she gave him a packet of ciggies or made him tea and gave him a 50p tip at the end of the day. He hated working for people who gave you zero at the end. There was no more work, and Marko thanked her politely and ran back down the stairs. He was employed by Community Services Industry, a local government organisation, which gave work to unemployed boys like Marko. The work consisted mainly of repairing and decorating corporation-owned apartments in the local area.

Trenchy saw Marko leave and peered up to the top floor. There was no sign of movement from flat two. He went out to wait on the steps.

Bicklo came out of the flat running. He always timed his jog down to work to a split second. On a Friday, however, he'd leave earlier than usual so that he could savour the anticipation of the six o'clock pay-packet that much longer. It was going to be a long, pleasurable day. As he took the stairs, he pulled on a faded denim jacket which matched his jeans.

Dave Bickley was surprisingly small and light for a 'king'. He seldom walked anywhere. He either jogged or strutted. His chest curved out from the rest of his body, and more often than not his shirt was either wide open or completely off. In repose his face was ordinary, but when he grinned he managed to look a mischievous innocent. On his cheek, below the right eye, was a livid scar. Bicklo was one of eight children: he had four brothers and three sisters.

Bicklo would have passed Trenchy if he hadn't been called.

'Marko's just gone,' Trenchy announced.

Bicklo nodded. 'I know. He's been working up there for the last two days. Not that I seen him. I heard.'

'He's looking all right,' Trenchy said.

'Not for long. I'll batter that nigger tonight.'

Bicklo ran out of James Place. He had a grudge against Marko. It was personal. Being a Bicklo in the territory was dangerous. If the niggers or the Dingle mob caught you they'd batter the shite out of you. His brother Harry had been walking along Windsor Street with sausage rolls for his boss, when Marko had caught him. Marko had knocked the rolls out of Harry's hands, stamped them into the pavement and then tried to batter his brother. Harry had run. Bicklo had vowed to get even.

He didn't look up at the cathedral as he jogged to Upper Parliament Street. Traffic was heavy, and Bicklo waited impatiently. Upper Parliament Street rises from the edge of the Mersey and runs straight east for a few miles up to Smithdown Lane. In the old days the poor lived at the bottom end; the rich from halfway up to the top. Today, it links Bicklo's territory to Marko's and parts of it are common territory.

Bicklo crossed 'Parly' to Rathbone Street, which was really a narrow, cobbled lane. At the Parly corner there stood the Stanley Arms; at the other end about three hundred yards away the lane petered out into waste ground. Bicklo passed the Liverpool University Settlement on the corner of Rathbone and Nile Streets. He stopped and looked up the slope of Nile Street. Two doors up, to the right, was his youth club, the Yorkie. Sometimes his spars would be hanging around the door even though the club only opened late afternoon. . . .

There are three main youth clubs that are patronised by the two gangs. York House is run by the Liverpool University Settlement, an independent organisation that survives on emoluments and grants, and apart from running the youth club it tries to help the local community by running adult literacy classes and a wide range of advisory services. The Yorkie is used exclusively by the Boot Boys.

The other two clubs are used by the black kids. On Great George Street, in a grimy, black-domed disused church, is the Great George project, known as the Blackie. At one time it was used by the white kids, for it's within their territory, but gradually the black kids took it over. It's financed by the Education Department, as is the newest youth club in Upper Parliament Street in the heart of the black area, the Robert Jones Community Centre, which is in the process of being built. It is run by the community as a self-help project. The three clubs are within half a mile of each other.

It was still too early though, and Nile Street was deserted. From Rathbone Street to the cathedral steps in St James's Road is only two hundred yards. It's a sad, cobbled stretch. Except for the club, the Settlement and one narrow house, all the buildings are deserted and abandoned. The windows are empty, black, glass-splintered sockets, the doors nailed corrugated sheets. Neglect and vandalism make them gaunt and haunted in appearance. Bicklo knew his way through their decaying guts like the back of his hand. He knew the broken roofs and the shattered stairs, the garbage-strewn backyards and alleys. It wasn't the only

8

street he knew well; he knew the whole territory. It was his kingdom, and he thought it a cool place in which to be born and to live. It stretched to Windsor Street in the east, west to the docks, north to the Black church and south towards the Dingle. There were only two things that bugged him. If the blacks had their own territory, he couldn't understand why some blacks still lived in his territory. He wished they'd move up the hill to join the others and leave his territory all white. And the same with the Roman Catholics. His hate for them was more deep-rooted than that for the niggers. Centuries of Irish history ran in his blood and moulded his mind.

Bicklo turned and ran alongside the iron-railed fence of the David Lewis. It was a large, neat, red-brick building that took up a whole block between Nile, Rathbone, Upper Parliament and Great George Streets. It housed an amalgam of activities. It had been built in the late nineteenth century by the founder of the David Lewis store, the largest department store in Liverpool, and remained a self-supporting charity. It ran a working-man's hostel to earn some of its money, and it also ran clubs for every age-group. 'From the cradle to the grave,' it boasted.

Bicklo bought ten No. 6 with the last of his money at the hostel's reception-desk. In Great George Street he glanced across to Upper Pitt Street, which stopped twenty yards short of Great George Street. The empty space between formed a triangle. On two sides were tenements, on the third Great George Street and railings. It was the regular meeting-place for him and his spars. It too was deserted.

On the corner of Great George Street were the Nelson, the Midland Bank and a petrol station. A long time ago there'd been a picture house on the corner, not that Bicklo could remember it. So much had changed in the last decade, mostly for the worse. They'd demolished row upon row of houses, shops, pubs, for the through-way they were planning to run into the city centre. It never came, but the land remained ravaged.

Smiths is an old warehouse, a block up from Queen's Dock. Under the huge sign on its roof, it announces that furniture, at attractive discount-rates, is available within. Bicklo passed the Furnace pub. Every Friday evening, after being paid, he and the other lads working in Smiths would spend an hour celebrating in the Furnace.

John, Dick and Steve were already in the store room, sprawled inelegantly in leather armchairs swathed in nylon protective covers. The warehouse had a cool, damp smell mixed with the strong odours of factory-fresh wood, rubber and nylon.

'All right, Dave?' each of them asked in ritual greeting before returning to their morning papers.

'All right,' Dave replied. He lay down on a large double bed and lit a cigarette. Just by bouncing he could tell he was lying on quality springs. It was a 'lux' costing nearly two hundred and fifty sheets. One day he'd have a bed like this in his house instead of the cheap foam-rubber shite other people had. He glanced around: proud. He was apprenticing to be a furniture remover and he already knew his job.

Bicklo was lucky to have the job. There were few to be had in Liverpool and a job that included some form of training was even rarer. He'd had more than his fair share of luck. On leaving school the previous year, he'd written a good, clever letter to Spencer's, a local electrical engineering firm, asking for an apprenticeship. He laughed at how easy it had been. His parents had composed the letter, and Spencer's had called him for an interview, and given him a maths test which anyone could pass who could add two and two. He'd got the apprenticeship. It had been too easy, and Bicklo soon became too confident. He pushed his luck from the start. He was sixteen and had the world by its balls. The first time wasn't his fault. It was the fucking niggers. He'd been battling them one night on Windsor Street, leading his boys in the skirmishes with bricks and bottles. Suddenly a brick hit him in the face. He blacked out. When he came to, blood was pouring down his face, and his spars had to take him to the casualty department. He'd had to take a couple of days off. The next time he went missing, though, was for a Liverpool home-game. He was supposed to be at evening classes at 7.30, but kick-off was also 7.30. Anyway, he'd reasoned while he was at the game, the course that day was only stuff he already knew. Spencer's didn't agree. They fired him a month later. Ironically the final straw wasn't his fault. He'd been out on the wagon–the delivery van–when his boss asked him to move it. Bicklo thought he knew how to drive. He crashed it.

Bicklo had felt sad at leaving that apprenticeship. An old technician had given him an engineering handbook which cost thirty sheets twenty years ago. The book was worth at least sixty today. Bicklo tried not to think about that lost opportunity. There was nothing he could do and so he'd persuaded himself that this new job as a furniture remover was as good.

'Okay, Dave, we're out on the wagon this morning,' his boss, John, said. John was Foreman at Smiths. Bicklo found him strange. He was a slim, brooding man who had this habit of reading. Each day he'd bring in a different book. At first Bicklo had taken an interest because he wanted to get well in with John. He'd take the book, read the title aloud, open to a page and return it. He stopped after a week. Books held nothing for him.

Bicklo jumped up front next to John after they'd loaded the furniture into the wagon. He loved going out for these rides. The wagon turned from St James's Street onto Parly, and they passed Windsor Street. Windsor Street is one of the boundaries between black and white. It's a long, anonymous-looking street crowded with corporation blocks, small shops, a few pubs and two schools.

As always his curiosity increased. He had never set foot in any street past Windsor Street. If he did, he knew he'd get battered by the coons. There is a physical difference between the two territories. Whereas the white area is composed exclusively of tenement blocks, in the black area half the people live in tenement blocks and the other half inhabit those elegant mansions of the rich. Seedy, neglected now, split into apartments and rooms. Beyond the corner of Windsor Street, Parly is made up of these decaying mansions. There are countless clubs in the basements–the Nigerian club, the Somali club, the West Indian club, the Gladray. In the daylight they look deserted and dissipated.

The wagon passed the Robert Jones. Bicklo recognised some of the black kids on the steps–Jimmy, Carlos, Kaye. . . . If he'd had a fucking shotgun he'd have gone *booom* at that doorway and wiped out half the niggers. At the lights the wagon turned right on to Prince's Avenue and moved past the heart of the black ghetto, where the National and Westminster bank stood in incongruous splendour, all gleaming glass, concrete and steel. Behind it loomed the squat yet majestically delicate Greek church with its steel-mesh-protected stained-glass windows. There were a few black men standing around rapping. As the wagon passed Upper Stanhope Street Bicklo saw Marko. It was a glimpse–Marko standing outside the chippy with a couple of other niggers. . . .

Marko's headache had gone. Once he'd crossed Windsor Street his head had cleared magically. The bromide of security physically transformed him. He'd begun to swagger; he hung looser. His arms swung as he walked and his heels hit the pavement confidently. For the first time he felt the warmth of the morning sun, the quiet breeze coming up from the Mersey. His guts had uncoiled.

Marko was rapping when Bicklo passed. He was in a good mood. The day had started well. A delivery van parked in Carter Street had had its doors open. The driver, a honky, had shrugged when Marko gave him the eye. It was cool. He'd lifted a pack of twenty No. 6, three cokes and a bag of sweets. The cokes and sweets he'd handed out, the ciggies he'd kept and was generously handing them around too.

Marko liked to think of himself as very aware. There was always some opportunity to make money, to find a screw, if you kept your eyes and ears open. Money could be found lying in the streets. It just took someone as smart as him to be able to find it, And he searched hard. He spent all his time thinking how to make easy money. A lot of it. Not just a pack of ciggies. He was looking for the big screw or else some-t-h-i-n-g. It was there, it was there. Marko had a vague ambition of becoming an electrician. It really was only something to say when people in authority asked him what he wanted to do. He wasn't afraid of going to prison if he was caught. He knew what he'd do inside. He'd learn from the old lags, learn everything; and once he came out he'd be able to open the world with a corkscrew.

Marko moved off slowly along Upper Stanhope Street. The rap hadn't been important. Just about the price of drag . . . if the supply was going to stay good . . . who'd been gripped by the pigs lately.

The vital part of Upper Stanhope Street is only a hundred yards long. Within that short stretch was all the action. The gambling-shops, the Reform Club at the corner, the Monty Carlo chippy, the post office, the Somali restaurant and the two pubs, the Prince's Park and the Berkeley. Marko made his connections for drag outside the Prince's Park. The strip was empty at the moment. However, by midday it would be hot. There'd be a crowd outside the pubs, the races would be on, the big boys would be playing their card game on the steps of the abandoned house in Carter Street. And you could buy anything you wanted. Drag, a woman, a radio, stereo, telly, car, scooter. Anything.

Marko began to hurry. As it was pay-day the honky from the

Community Services would drop in at any time to check if he was working in the house. He had a wallpapering job to do on the ground floor of a Berkeley Walk flat. When he got to the house, Jim, a half-caste boy his own age, was hard at work. Marko and him were supposed to work as a team. Jim always did; Marko preferred to cruise the territory. Parky, the thin, pot-bellied Trinidadian in immediate charge was watching television.

At one time, Parky had been a really big man. He'd owned six nightclubs! On Saturday nights when he went to the Masonic Arms in Great George Street to hear the sounds of local groups, his drinking friends would remember those clubs. They'd also remember, painfully to Parky, that, according to local legend, he was another one of those–and there must be many in the world–who refused to rehire the Beatles after their one-night gig in his club.

'You know what Parky done la?' they'd say. 'He told the Beatles that they should go away and learn how to play music.' They'd laugh at Parky, and he'd try to laugh with them.

'Man, I'm telling you they couldn't play,' he'd reply. They'd shake their heads. To have held such vast magic briefly in the palm of your hand . . . hot, man, hot . . . juicy with money . . . and then *thrown* it out. Nor could they understand how you could lose six nightclubs. Parky had liked his booze too much, and the clubs had disappeared. Now he was a handyman. If you needed your window fixed, your carpet laid, your wall papered, you called on Parky. And if he needed anyone to mix the paint or hold the ladder he'd call Marko. Parky liked Marko and thought him a smart boy–except for one thing. Marko hated white people, and this puzzled Parky. After all, Marko was Liverpudlian and half-caste. At nights when he was drunk, Parky would think about Marko. He decided he was going to teach Marko to like white people, the way he did. It was too easy to hate, Parky would say to himself, and difficult to love. He would spend the next three years, he calculated, showing Marko that white people weren't evil. Parky couldn't know that it was already too late.

Marko handed a ciggie to Parky and the woman who lived in the flat. She was plump and attractive with a half a dozen different-looking half-caste children. She saw one of them sucking on a coke.

'Where'd you get that?' she demanded.

'From a wagon,' the boy said. She snatched the bottle from him.

13

'If I catch you stealing again, I'll kill you,' she threatened. It was all she could do, threaten. It was impossible to control the children when you lived in the area. Once they went out of the door there was no chance of knowing where they'd be or what they'd do.

'Better get to work, Ivor,' Parky said. 'The man'll be coming some time this morning, and if he catches you doing nothing I'm not going to help you.'

Marko picked up a roll of wood-patterned paper. The woman wanted her flat to look panelled. He didn't get further than the foot of the stairs. Ato was leaning against the wall rapping with Carlos. Marko, with the roll in one hand and a brush in the other, hesitated. Ato waved. Marko went across.

'Haven't seen you for some time la,' Marko said.

'I been at home,' Ato said. He looked worried. In fact so worried that he'd forgotten he wasn't supposed to be talking to Marko. They'd argued a week ago and sworn never to be friends. 'It's really evil at home la.'

'What's it?' Marko asked.

Ato shook his head. 'Can't tell you la. You wouldn't like it.'

'Gettin' pressure?'

'You can call it that,' Ato said. He wouldn't say more, and after a long awkward silence added: 'Later la.'

He wandered disconsolate down Berkeley Walk towards Upper Stanhope Street. From where he stood, he could look back and see nothing but council houses. The estate was fairly new. The oldest building was ten years old, the newest was still being built. In spite of its newness, the whole estate looked dishevelled. Garbage remained uncollected; the windows in the stairwells were broken; graffiti decorated most of the walls.

Ato pouted in worry, and his fingers fidgeted. They kept wanting to scratch, and he'd try to control them. Only for a moment, and then his fingers would start exploring his skin.

Ato was big for seventeen. There was a bony width to his body, and he walked as if he were marching to a tune running in his head. His skin was white and smooth as any honky's. You could see the delicate blue veins on his hands and face. His hair alone distinguished him from the honkies. It was gingerish blonde and tightly, tightly curled. At times he would tug angrily at it. He wanted very much to grow an Afro like Marko's, but his hair was just too tight to grow long. His features matched his hair. He had heavy cheekbones, flared nostrils and thick lips.

14

It had taken him years to accept himself as black. He was so near to the other side that as a child he'd persuaded himself he was really white. If only, he'd thought, he could change his hair and his face. The kids in Arundel Comprehensive began calling him names. 'Ato, you white coon . . . Ato, you honky nigger.' He'd asked his mother to explain, and cryptically she'd told him you are what you are. As he grew older he began to understand. He now wished his skin was black instead of this horrible white; he wished he were African. A student, studying in Liverpool who would one day return home to his country, to his language, to his culture. He was only black now because they wouldn't let him be anything else; and he wasn't sure what that really meant. He still had troubles. When he fought the Boot Boys, they'd jeer at him: 'Hey, Ato, what's a white boy like you doing with those niggers.' Ato would point to his hair. When they continued to call, he'd pull on it to show it was kinky. Pull harder and harder, and the Boys would laugh louder.

Ato fidgeted as he stood in Upper Stanhope Street. He wanted to return home and bathe. The day had begun badly for him. Friday usually made him feel powerfully good. It was the start of the weekend. There'd be a shebeen somewhere, a card-game, some good drag and maybe some good pussy to grind. But this morning he'd woken with an itch. He lived with his mother and two sisters in the centre flat of a decrepit house on Cairns Street. Below them was a bowling-ball maker, and the flat above was empty. During term university students rented it, and Ato would often spend nights with them smoking drag and listening to sounds. Ato had a room to himself. Sometimes his younger brother, who lived with his aunt in Wales because of his asthma, would return briefly to share the room. As this wasn't often, Ato called it his room.

The itch, when he had first noticed it, was on his chest. The skin was red and slightly broken. Ato had immediately switched on the record-player. Osibisa was his favourite. Music sometimes made him feel secure; it was his music, black sounds. He had huge posters of Isaac Hayes, Rap Brown, the Supremes; there wasn't a honky face on any wall. Opposite the bed was a small bookcase, full of books that were all sci-fi. Osibisa should have soothed him. It didn't. His sanctuary had been invaded. He needed desperately to confess of this sin that had visited him.

15

2

ATO thought of confessing to Marko; Marko would understand. No, he wouldn't. There were some things in life a man couldn't tell even his spar. Marko would shun him; Carlos would shun him; they'd all push him out of their lives once they knew.

Kaye was sitting on the wall outside the Chinese chippy, and Ato joined him. He knew there'd be silence and time to think about his problem. Kaye never talked much. The light-grey eyes in the young black face always looked calm. He seemed shy and quiet, but Ato knew better. Kaye just didn't think much. Ato didn't see much of Kaye. Nobody did, as Kaye spent most of his time in remand homes. He'd just come out of one after doing eighteen months for taking and driving a car; previously he'd been in for taking and driving a scooter and burglary.

'You heard?' Kaye asked.

'What?' Ato didn't say it with conviction. He wasn't interested.

'Some beef got the shite beaten out of herself outside the Alex last night,' Kaye said with relish. The Alexander was a pub at the bottom of Gibson Street and a stone's throw from Upper Stanhope Street.

'No, I didn't hear,' Ato confessed. It was surprising, as news, no matter how trivial, travels fast and silently through the ghetto. Ato hadn't heard the whispers because he was too preoccupied. The details were commonplace. A prostitute had had her face booted in, and had lain for hours outside the pub before the police found her. It was all in the *Liverpool Post*, Kaye said. Briefly Ato was interested. The whores hung out outside the Alex and along Granby Street. The two boys remembered that during the 1972 fighting between the blacks and whites the black kids had taken to protecting the whores. The kids resented honky motorists cruising their streets looking for black pussy. They'd stopped the cars by hurling bricks through the windscreens or else battering any honky that got out to approach a whore. Those were good times la.

'Later,' Ato said and trudged the few yards up to Parly. His forehead was ridged with a thick frown. He kicked a coke can for a few steps, indifferent to the noise. He passed the haberdasher, Watson, and nodded in greeting.

Watson was a big Jamaican who always wore a cap with a plastic peak. He was in his normal pose–leaning on the counter looking out. He'd only owned the shop a few weeks and business was still shaky. He'd bought it from an old white lady for two hundred pounds; and even that, he felt, was too much as she'd deliberately ruined her business. He didn't understand people sometimes. Here was this white lady who owned a store in a black area, and instead of trying to get along with the people she'd antagonise them. When a black girl wanted to buy a black pullover or black panties or black wool, the white lady would make sarcastic remarks about the girl's love for black. He shook his head. That was no way to run a business, man. You had to get on. Especially with half-caste kids like Ato.

If you didn't, they could give you a lot of pressure. People are like animals, Watson would say; they sense when you're afraid of them, when you dislike them. The white lady had hated the half-caste kids, and they knew it. One day they poked an iron-tipped stick through the steel mesh protecting the window and smashed the expensive plate-glass. Watson didn't pressure the kids. He'd let them lean against his car; it was better than chasing them away. One man had chased the kids, and they'd thrown a brick through the windscreen. The kids let Watson alone.

Still, it was getting worse every day. He'd lived in the area for nearly fifteen years. Five years at the beginning when he'd first arrived from Jamaica. Then he'd emigrated to Newark, New Jersey, United States, and that had been good. He'd worked hard, eaten and slept. That was the way to save money, and in America there was money. Unfortunately, his wife hadn't liked America and they'd returned to another ten years in the area. He no longer lived there now. He could see the ghetto rising. It was becoming like Harlem, and each day the violence seemed to increase. He saw a lot through the narrow aperture of the doorway. Last week he'd seen three lads mug a man coming out of the bank across the road. They'd been waiting for him for some time. Like most of the older generation, Watson just couldn't understand why the black kids hated the white people. You lived with them; you didn't have to trust them, but you got on. There was no alternative.

Ato sat on the steps of the Rialto furniture-store at the corner of Berkeley Street and Parly. The Rialto had been a cinema eight years ago; three years back Councillor Swainbank had turned it into a huge furniture-store.

Ato submerged into his fantasies. His favourite was that he was surrounded by this aura at least two feet away from his body. It wrapped him in warmth with a large human-shaped glow of light, shimmering and steel hard, which nobody could pierce. When he was standing in the aura he felt himself grow bigger and stronger; it gave him such power over the whole world that every command of his was obeyed. It made him feel . . . God. Sometimes, he was a spaceman on a different planet; a world far better than earth.

Like most of his friends, Ato devoured sci-fi. It depicted a workless, poorless, adventurous world, a world filled with strange creatures, marvellous machines and endless possibilities. It was a tomorrow world which changed from book to book. It was far better than reading stories about today, about the world he existed in; in those stories he could recognise the people, the problems, the events, and they all frightened him. In sci-fi he could move surely, calmly through the pages knowing that there was nothing to harm or disillusion him.

Fantasy, whether sci-fi or self-delusion, is necessary to Ato as to everyone else who inhabits the two territories. It is a giant hypodermic, thrust into their brains and slowly draining out their real vision. If you held the syringe up to the sun, the liquid would not be bright with colour. It would be grey and dull and crowded with the countless, wriggling microbes of their fears. No light would reflect off it; no light would pass through it. In this liquid would also be the sinews of their minds, the mental muscle that should help them to confront the world. Each day the pressure increases, the syringe draws out more of the sinew, sucking it out pleasurably until in its place is left a dark, warm void. A tiny hollow in the centre that gradually enlarges to the size of a fist. Like the wounds inflicted on a boxer by his opponents' savagery, so the poor have the wound in their heads. It's been there for centuries, a self-perpetuating wound that passes through the bellies of the women who bear them, and only the very few ever escape its contamination. They manage to heal themselves temporarily as they scramble out of the tenements. The healing is only temporary.

One flick of the scalpel of insecurity and the wound bleeds again. Those who remain fill the hollow with fantasies which, like soft acid, eat further into the tissues until, too weak, they succumb to their inertia.

For Ato, the ju-ju worked. It pushed away the ill omen that had woken him this morning and in ten minutes he felt fine. He remembered it was Friday. The good day when people begin to smile again in anticipation of the weekend. Ato smiled too. He grinned and jumped up. He sauntered up Parly towards the Robert Jones.

He passed the Pony Express café. At the pinball machine were a few boys; no one was at the slot machine. Seated near the entrance were half a dozen Somalis, handsome men. Their black, delicate faces had long, fine noses, and they looked like gazelles. The Somalis held themselves aloof from both the white people and the black people, including Nigerians, Ghanaians and other African races. Like the Bedouin they were proud, and it showed in the way they'd look at you. Two years ago, there'd been a battle between them and the West Indians. A man was killed, and the Somali club bombed. Since then they'd withdrawn further. There were only a few of them, maybe a hundred. In the mornings they met in the Pony Express, run by Akhmed, afternoons in the Blue Moon Somali restaurant in Upper Stanhope Street, and in the evenings in the Somali club, diagonally opposite the Pony Express.

Ato felt in his pockets. He had no money for the pinball. It didn't worry him; he'd be paid today. He passed Cliff's winestore, the chemist, and Irene's hairdressing salon. He looked into Liverpool Personnel, and saw Geraldine bent over her typewriter. Next to L.P. was the Robert Jones, spread over three rambling old mansions. Ato ran up the stairs to start work.

Bicklo climbed out of the wagon cautiously to stand and stare at the house, which stood well back from the road on a tree-lined avenue near Sefton Park. It was a large, imposing house built around the 1840s. Its walls were ivy-covered, and it looked dignified and solid. Bicklo was also awed by the two cars standing in the drive. One was a Bentley, the other a Jag. He approached the Bentley and peered in. He'd never seen one close at hand; they didn't park Bentleys in Great George Street. He sniffed. The odour of leather and perfume was alien. He wasn't sure what to think about the car. It stood there, so real, yet he was sure it would suddenly disappear if he touched it. He did and left a thumb-print on the handle.

'Come on, Dave,' John called. 'I want this lot in by dinner.'

Bicklo trotted back to the wagon, helped John unload the furniture and carry it into the house. He didn't see the people who inhabited the house. As with the car, he didn't really believe they existed. However, he saw the wealth. It was mesmeric. Brass . . . pictures on the walls . . . and a piano . . . and leather chairs . . . and 'lux' carpets . . . and polished wood tables . . . and decanters . . . and bookcases. He would never be able to explain what he saw; it was as if he'd walked into a pharaoh's tomb. Later he tried to tell Chas about the fireplace. It was all marble la, he said, and . . . and . . . big marble. He couldn't capture the magnificence.

'Fucking brass la . . . fucking leather chairs . . . this piano.' He would stop and try to remember, but it had all begun to fade. He had to forget it, in self-defence. It couldn't exist within him and allow him to survive for long. It would suffocate him, so instinctively he forgot.

Now, as he worked with John in the bedroom, he touched things. The fragile chairs, the coverlets on the beds, the velvet curtains. They felt strange, cool and almost electric. There was money lying on the dresser. Bicklo moved to it. He fingered the fivers. He would have loved to pocket the money but he knew it wasn't worth his job. He cursed.

It made him frustrated and angry. He could never, never, imagine what it was like to be rich; he knew he would never be rich. The poor have no idea how rich the rich are; the rich have no care how poor the poor are. Bicklo was at this moment as bewildered by what he saw and felt and smelt as those sadly doomed savages in some distant country who first saw a white man. The world that Bicklo lived in and the one he now stood in were as far apart as that first confrontation between alien cultures. The culture that he, Dave Bickley, King of the Park Street Boot Boys, represented, was far simpler than the one he now beheld. His culture had the same complexities as that of primitive man. The ritual of tribe, the ritual of battle, the ritual of courtship, the ritual of superstition, the ritual of work. He had little art with which to express himself. Maybe some music and dancing, but no paintings, no stone carvings.

Bicklo, in this confrontation, sees only the wealth. The brass, the carpets, the piano. He doesn't understand that behind this façade lie the sinews of power. Wealth, to the middle and upper classes, is only the by-product of their search for power and control. The economic power of the owner of this house, be he a doctor, an engineer, a lawyer, a professor, accumulates until it finally becomes social and political power. The three strings with which he can manipulate and control Bicklo. The poor have no means of understanding this power. They are taught the minutiae of money–the wage-packet, the rent, the pension–and because of this brutally amputated vision they can only reach for immediate fulfilment, believing that money is the cure for their condition.

The power is manifested briefly to Bicklo when he stands in the court in front of a magistrate, who owns a house similar to this one, and who causes this young king, now shorn of all his own little power, to hold one hand raised high in the air while the court is in session. This is done to humiliate him in front of the pigs, the lawyers, his parents, his friends; to reveal to the boy that the man on the bench holds greater power than Bicklo. The humiliation makes Bicklo only angry, not humble.

His anger is mixed with frustration. He wants not only to possess all this that he sees, convertible into quick money: the brass a fiver, the piano maybe twenty–he doesn't even know the value of the objects he wants to steal–but also to destroy what he cannot plunder. He once broke into a house, similar to this one, near his territory. It wasn't as wealthy but still belonged to this alien culture. He broke the meter for money, took a few brass plates, and then he ravaged the house like some big stud bursting open the tender womb of a fragile girl. He opened the fridge and hurled all the bottles against the vinyl tile, sunset pastel-coloured walls; he smashed the antique coffee-tables; he shoved his boot through the twenty-four-inch, colour, multi-channel television; he tore the velvet curtains from their poles; he smashed a chair into the hall mirror, ripped the coverlets of the beds. The destruction was brief, terrible and awesome. He was sweating when he'd finished and he was satisfied. He had reduced the wealth and order to the shambles of his own life. The shattered china and stained walls somehow made an equation he could understand. Their world wasn't made of a steel he couldn't bend or break; it was human like his own.

Bicklo moved away from the pile of notes. As he worked, he fantasised that it was he who lived in the house. Not as big. Though he stood in it he still couldn't imagine such a big place for himself. His fantasy was limited to a council house, a mini and enough money to get the beef when he wanted, to drink when he wanted, to buy the gear when he wanted. It was simple, yet so unattainable.

He was earning twelve pounds a week. By the time he paid his mother for food, bought ciggies, a beer, it was all gone. There was nothing to spend until the next Friday.

They finished by dinner. The middle-aged, distant woman in the house tipped them each a whole pound. Bicklo liked her briefly for that, though he couldn't imagine how she could afford two pounds. On the drive back, he was silent for a long time.

'You seen many places like that John?' Bicklo finally asked.

'A few.'

'Shite. Wish I could have that money la.'

'You've got no chance Dave, unless you rob a bank. I don't let it worry me. I've got enough for my needs.'

Bicklo had wanted to be reassured that he wasn't the only one that envied. In this John failed. But John was different; he was, if Bicklo had known the word, an aesthete. He didn't, so he decided John was strange and didn't need money. Only those books.

The wagon turned into Prince's Avenue. It was really two tree-shaded, one-way avenues with a broad, sandy promenade between the traffic lanes. There were quite a few more black people around; strolling, sitting under the shade of the trees, rapping. Upper Stanhope Street looked busy as the wagon whizzed past and turned on to Parly. Marko was sauntering into Liverpool Personnel. Bloody hell, he never works, does he, Bicklo thought.

Marko was on another skive and checking to see if Geraldine had any apple pie to give him.

Liverpool Personnel . is an employment agency. It is a non-profit-making organisation which specialises in placing black people in jobs and helping school-leavers to choose careers and training programmes. Its aims are politically ambitious–nothing less than to change the attitudes not only of employers in Liverpool, but also of local government. Very ambitious: the local authorities prefer to believe there is no black problem; the employers prefer to believe there are no black people. Out of every hundred black people who come to L.P. in search of jobs, only twenty succeed. The skilled ones find jobs as ship's cooks or in restaurants after taking a catering course at Liverpool College, others, after training, as spray painters or mechanics. These are very few. The majority have to work as porters, dish-washers, cleaners, and even these jobs are hard to find because of the

22

employment situation in Liverpool and the employers' preference for white employees.

L.P. did bring cases to the Race Relations Board. Marko had been one of their causes. He had gone for a job as a porter in a boutique. The manager told Marko that the job would be too hard and dirty for him–as if looking at Marko he saw a lily-white faggot dressed in a shining mohair suit and a raw silk cream shirt! L.P. lost the case. There were many firms so subtle in their rejection that no case could be proved. L.P. would play their game. They'd first send a black man. He'd be told the job had been taken. Then they'd send a white man, who would be hired.

In immediate charge of Liverpool Personnel is a white, middle-class woman, Sue Shafer. Marko likes her, even though she comes from an alien civilisation. More important than liking, Marko trusts her, as do most black people in the ghetto. She isn't a liberal who gives a blanket love to black people, though ever since her university days she has been among the first people to organise the anti-apartheid movement in England.

SUE SHAFER: *'If you're a white person in daily contact with black people, they expect you to give them 110-per-cent approval before they're willing to accept you. I try to keep a balance and take them as individuals, and I'm not afraid of telling them their faults to their faces. A lot of black people have a romantic view of themselves–cool, hip, and other myths–which is totally distorted.*

'Apart from the trouble we have with firms and the local government, the kids themselves have no idea what they really want to do. You've got to suggest things and hope they'll be interested, and then you find they don't want to leave the ghetto and all their friends. A lot of them also don't like one of them to become better, so in order to stay with their friends they slip back into the pit–dead-end jobs, no jobs, police records. Do you know that quite a few black children request to be transferred to other schools because of the environment. They can't study, they can't show any interest in their courses because their friends will make fun of them. It's their only chance to succeed, to escape the pit.'

With Sue in L.P. are Perry Lee, a half-caste Chinese boy, and Geraldine Williams, a half-caste black girl. Though Sue is the one with ultimate responsibility, she hates anyone even jocularly to call Perry and Geraldine her assistants.

Perry is in his early twenties and has moved from Liverpool's

Chinatown, where he was born, to live nearer the ghetto. He had always wanted to do some kind of social work and he was happy to be in L.P. If he'd stayed down in Chinatown he'd have run a Chinese chippy or else, like his brother, clashed with the pigs.

Geraldine is a pretty girl with deep grey eyes. She'd met Sue on a bus and Sue hadn't treated her as a black person. Like most of the girls in the ghetto, Geraldine had gone straight from school at fifteen into a factory job. She'd wanted to study for O Levels, but her mother needed the money. Geraldine thought that if she worked hard enough and made herself liked she would be promoted in her factory to the job of supervisor. For the first year, she'd always arrived on time, worked very hard, much harder than all the honky workers, and at the end of the year she waited for promotion. She was *that* innocent of life. She was fired when she asked why she wasn't promoted. She threatened to report the factory to the Race Relations Board and they rehired her as a supervisor, but still doing the same job as before. She left, and after that she drifted. She would try initially to work hard and then give up each time. They only wanted an animal, not a person.

Sue was looking for a black girl when they met. A special girl who hadn't yet become too bitter and who wanted desperately to learn. L.P. was the first decent job Geraldine had ever had and she was determined to succeed. She was taking her O Levels and she knew she was lucky. Other girls her age had either become hookers by now or else married and had kids.

Marko spent ten minutes in L.P. Geraldine gave him a slice of pie and he bummed a cigarette off Sue. They were both soft on him; most people were, because he looked so vulnerable. All three of them gave Marko special treatment. In a day maybe fifty people would come to Liverpool Personnel to drink coffee, to talk about a job, to swear at the honky bastards, some just to rest their feet and stare out of the window. When Marko came, all three would stop to ask how he was. They felt a sadness for him, for unlike the others there seemed to be reserved for Marko a special doom. He was already standing on the edges of danger. He was too well known to the Boot Boys to last unharmed for long; he was too well known to the pigs to stay out of trouble for long.

They were both waiting. He had already been caught for burglary and 'affray' and convicted; he had been given suspended sentences and been placed on probation.

Marko hurriedly drank his coffee. The finger from Social

24

Security would be in Berkeley Walk any moment with his wages. He scorched out of the door and saw Ato. Ato had paint over his hair and clothes. He and another boy were fencing with paint brushes.

'You goin' to buy some drag later?' Marko asked.

'I don't get paid till the evening la,' Ato said. 'One minute. I'll hustle some bread from Bobby.'

'Okay. You come and pick me up and we'll get fucking stoned.' Marko scorched.

Ato leapt in the air and screamed, 'Stoned la. Absolutely fucking stoned by three o'clock.' He ran into the Robert Jones to hustle Bobby or anyone else he could find. It was Friday. Everyone was waiting for their pay.

The Robert Jones wasn't completed. Early in 1973 William Sefton, chairman of Liverpool Corporation, gave the three rambling houses to the community for their self-help project. It was still cluttered with paint cans, step-ladders and repair equipment. Ato and a dozen other unemployed boys work in the Jones as painters and decorators. Bobby Nyahoe, a young black man, was until lately the project-leader. He's an articulate, bouncy, likeable man with a scar on his nose where he was once bitten in a fight. He is a mixture of publicist and politician and quite often humorously aware of his own shortcomings. He calls himself at times a Barclaycard revolutionary.

Bobby had been born in the ghetto and had hustled his way through life. For years he could never imagine life as anything but a physical hustle, fighting, stealing, staying above the line just long enough to catch a burst of air. He was also one of the first registered drug addicts in Liverpool. The irony of it was that it was his drug life that made him go straight. As a drug addict, he tells you, you meet a better class of people than those who live in the ghetto. Writers, painters, middle-class hippies who lived in a different civilisation to the one he grew up in. It was this contact which straightened out his mind. He began to read, learn and think. He lives outside the ghetto now with his white wife and son in a suburb of Liverpool.

The Robert Jones is the first experiment in self-help, and no middle-class, white administrator gives the orders. Bobby runs the centre with the help of people who live in the area. Albert, Cliff, Ramon, Caroline and Sandra are black; Frank, Dixie and John Henshaw, the warden, are white. Apart from the Jones not being physically ready, there are other problems. Without that deeply ingrained, white, middle-class work-ethic, the people who run the Jones are often undisciplined. Sometimes they're

25

there; sometimes not. Sometimes the work gets done; often it's left undone for weeks. It's the first time they've been given the opportunity to administer and control and it's very difficult without the training. There are so many complexities that the middle class have an almost instinctive knowledge of: administration, accounting, delegation, punctuality; discipline. The poor have no practice at these middle-class virtues in their lives.

Down by those docks not more than a mile away, the iron rings to which the black slaves were chained are still embedded in the walls. They've been there four centuries, rusted with the sweat of the palms of those black men and women who clutched them in pain and despair. If the rings could have been broken and twisted, they would have been snapped like dry twigs. The slaves were in transit to America and the West Indies, and as they held the rings they were branded with the initials of their once-famous owners. The rings and the walls are impregnated with their screams. ST ... DD ... M ... K. Brands of quality merchandise. The glowing curved irons possessively burnt the tender flesh of their foreheads, their arms, their buttocks, their bellies. As they smelt the odour of singed flesh and felt the voltage shocks of pain, they screamed. The scream carried back over the vast ocean to their villages deep in Africa, and forward in time through the centuries. Sending shock waves through the souls of those still yet to come, still unborn; piercing them through the cosmic umbilical cord so that they emerged from the womb, screaming and branded the same way as their chained and long-dead ancestors.

The delay in completing the Robert Jones isn't solely the fault of Bobby and his team. As with all the other youth projects in the city, there is never enough money from the Education Department. In an education budget of £2 million, only £20,000 is set aside for the youth clubs and community services. At a meeting held by the three youth clubs—the Yorkie, the Blackie and the Robert Jones—patronised by the street-fighting gangs, all those present were aware they were reaching a crisis. The Blackie was due to close down for much-needed redecoration; the Robert Jones wasn't ready. That left the Yorkie; and the Yorkie was Bicklo's club, and they doubted he'd let the black kids use it.

'Look la, the only answer is that you get the Jones working,' John Warren, of the Yorkie, told Bobby. 'There'll be a riot if the black kids use the Yorkie.'

'How do I get it working la?' Bobby asked. 'There's no time left and I

26

don't have the money. It's taken me weeks just to get the disco working. You send in a requisition to the Education Department for lights for the disco and you never hear from them for months. You know that as well as I do. If you keep the Yorkie open longer, this'll keep the white kids off the streets.'

'How the hell can I?' John asked. 'There are only four of us. We're open in the afternoon during the holidays and every evening, except the weekends.'

'Open on Saturday and Sunday,' Bobby said.

'For God's sake, we need a rest now and then,' Bill said. 'We're working the whole time.'

'Working?' Wendy said. She and her husband, Bill Harp, ran the Blackie with a large team of youth workers. Of the three clubs, the Blackie is the most efficiently run. Apart from being the jewel in the Education Department's crown of youth clubs, it was managed by the middle class for the poor. 'We're open six days a week, and on the seventh we have our weekly meeting to organise the next week. None of us gets any rest. If you don't open twenty-four hours a day, the kids want to know why. If you do, they want it open twenty-six hours.'

'If we all bug the Education Department together,' Bobby suggested, 'maybe they'll give us more money and speed everything up.'

'The only time we'll get more money is when the kids start rioting,' Wendy said. 'Then we'll get lots and quickly because the Press will be covering the fighting.'

They joked for a while about starting the kids rioting so that they could lever more money out of the Education Department. They stopped soon and brooded. They were tired. Summer would be finishing soon and the long, dreary winter lay ahead. They worried mostly about the Robert Jones. It was moving too slowly; and the pressure was increasing. Wendy and a few of the other youth workers would spend their spare time working in the Jones. They'd built the large inflatable in the back hall; they'd show movies in the afternoons; they'd try to advise. They knew they couldn't do more: it was Bobby's project after all.

Apart from money and time there was one more pressure on the youth workers. The kids. They were fickle. One evening they'd crowd the half-completed disco in the Robert Jones; then for a week no one would enter the building. One day there'd be 150 kids down in the Blackie; the next a mere thirty. They were unpredictable in their likes and dislikes and brutally unaware that all Bobby's and Wendy's and John's efforts were solely for their benefit. The pressure the youth workers had was dreaming up new entertainments, new enticements. Like the missionaries they were, sent by the Great Society and their own calling, the youth workers were there to save the souls of these new savages. The sermon they preached was not fire and damnation and a bland hereafter, for it wasn't the Devil they were saving the savages from. It was the police. Even victory was brief. The kids would put pressure again. Wanting the club open longer, wanting more movies, wanting, always wanting. The alternative was the street corner.

Ato, like Bobby and John Warren, knew the street corner well. You could drift into anything on the corner with a few spars–a burglary, a fight, anything. The permutation was not unlimited, only dangerous for the kids. Whatever way it started, it ended, nearly always, in a police cell.

At seventeen, Ato had already done fourteen months in reform school for breaking and entering. It was a stupid screw. He'd done many others before: car radios, tapes, sweets, little nothings which had no value beyond the thrill of theft. For some he'd been caught and placed on probation, but never sent to reform school until this one. He had been stoned that evening and remembered vaguely staggering home at four in the morning. Then for some reason he decided to break into a house quite near his place. It was really stupid. He couldn't control his mind or his body and it was too near home. The neighbours heard him stumbling around and called the police. When he came out of reform, Ato vowed to himself he'd stay out of trouble until he was twenty-one. But he didn't get the chance.

One evening he'd been drinking in the Masonic pub in Great George Street, which was patronised mainly by black people. As he'd stepped into the street, four Skinheads approached him.

'You Ato,' they asked.

Ato knew the tone of voice. He'd heard it often in dozens of cowboy movies, on street corners in gangster movies, on street corners in his own life. He ran. They tripped him before he'd taken four steps. The boots came in fast, before he'd even hit the pavement; sinking and skidding off his ribs and sides. He saw the jagged bottle coming down on his face and blocked it with his right hand. In a moment, his face was drenched with the blood pumping from his sliced wrist. The glass, he discovered later, had cut the artery and the muscles. For six months he couldn't use the hand until the doctors stitched the muscles together. Ato waited for his revenge. He managed to catch one of the boys and beat the shite out of him. Now he waited for the others.

It was the street corner that had lost him time in reform school and scarred his hand for life. Just by being part of an amorphous mass of forty to fifty boys and girls, he couldn't help but find trouble. There were no leaders, as in the American gangs, to control and channel them. There was no gang life, no generals, lieutenants, rituals, initiations. It was just an unco-ordinated mass.

Only once had organisation touched their lives profoundly. In 1972 they adopted Black Power. Apart from one or two of the older boys, who became the leaders, none of them read much philosophy. What had reached them across the Atlantic was the image. The leather coats, the dark glasses, the clenched fist raised in salute. For the first time they belonged to something and it gave them a brief and exhilarating sense of identity. It wasn't only the uniforms–brown leather jackets–but also the knowledge that across the ocean were a people similar to themselves. A black population, like themselves the descendants of slaves, besieged in a white country, with no country of their own to return to.

Whenever Ato thought about that year he'd feel the excitement again. The older boys, now in prison, had organised the kids. Bill Johns, one of the leaders, had been gripped by the pigs while travelling in a car with a boot full of petrol bombs. It had been a cool time. Bill had formed the Black Panther Party and the Black Panther Men, in all about ninety boys, and the big press from London had come to write about them. Every evening they'd form up, with leaders for each squad, and march down to the old cathedral grounds. They'd train and practise combat for an hour or two in the evening gloom. Scaling walls, sprinting, physical jerks, attacks, defence. Like faint shadows, always one step behind, they followed the movements of the American Black Panthers. They readied their ninety young vibrant bodies for the moment of revolution that they knew would come one day. They would be the shock troops of the war and their muscles would, magically, turn to iron and steel. To an observer standing in Hope Street looking down at the kids preparing for war it must have been a sad sight. One hundred of them–against a machine that could annihilate them at the flick of a finger. There *was* an observer watching the games, for when the time came the police unerringly picked out the leaders.

The joy, however, could not be stolen from them. That moment

29

of common identity had shifted and hardened them; they began to understand the politics of their colour. There were some who had loved it for the promise of violence, the chance to release the blind, bewildering rage that had been bottled up for so long. For others it was the first time they were aware that they were black Liverpudlians with no country to call their own. The white blood in their veins stopped at the threshold of their mother's womb; the black was a new route still to be explored.

Bobby wanted to use the Robert Jones to teach some of this history. It wasn't only going to be a play centre for the kids but a place to learn what they were never taught in schools. How can a black kid, he would ask, identify with Henry VIII, Napoleon and Winston Churchill. He wanted the kids to have black heroes who would not disillusion them when the time came. School only fostered the white myths, and played down the black man. Bobby gave interviews to the Press demanding black schools, a black university, and this worried the city leaders. They couldn't understand what was wrong with Churchill as a hero to a nigger boy. He was fine for them.

3

TRENCHY was depressed. He was sitting in a draughty classroom overlooking Windsor Street. St Martin's was nicknamed the open air school because nearly every window had been broken in the battling between the Boot Boys and the black kids. The bill for broken windows alone came to £750 a year.

Trenchy, like Bobby, thought there was everything wrong with school. All he could see ahead of him was one year of life to be wasted. He should have been outside working with Bill Lacey. Lacey was a fifty-five-year-old odd-job man and a friend of Trenchy's father; he'd promised Trenchy that when he finished school he would take him on as an apprentice. But it was getting too late for that, for Lacey had arthritis and was thinking of retiring this year. Without him, Trenchy wasn't sure what to do for a job when he left school. His father worked as a labourer on a building site and, though he was now a foreman, he had little power to get Trenchy on to a site. Not that he wanted his son to be a labourer.

Trenchy had decided three years ago that he and school were totally incompatible. He had been doing well until he came to that decision. His parents were proud of his marks, and his behaviour and attendance had been exemplary. But, that was three years ago. It was the era of the Skinheads, and all the boys except Trenchy had shorn their hair close to the skull. The difference in hair-length didn't exclude Trenchy from their ranks. One day, Mr Currie, the deputy headmaster, called Trenchy a Skinhead. Trenchy had always disliked Currie, and this was the worst insult possible.

The remark was no better or worse than any other made by a teacher to a boy but it triggered Trenchy towards destruction. Up till then he'd been balanced on a knife edge between being good and bad. The remark toppled him. From that day on he sulked

31

and, like a monk doing penance as a sign of his martyrdom, began to grow his hair. It was shoulder-length now, and even his mother's pleas refused to make him cut it. He took it out on himself in many other ways. In inflicting punishment on himself, Trenchy thought Currie would also feel the pain. He stopped studying. His marks, from being above average, became the worst; he played truant whenever he could; he fought with boys and the teachers. Trenchy's mother, aware of her son's self-destructiveness, went to see Currie, and asked him to retract the statement. He did, but it made no difference. The damage had been done. Trenchy, like the other boys, lives very near the surface of his skin. There is nothing deep and hidden and secure; no point of strength that will help him in life. Currie had gouged through the thin skin, and there was no pulling back on the knife. Trenchy wanted it embedded, to force Currie to carry the burden of guilt for having destroyed a boy by a careless crack.

Trenchy's life is constructed of such minute acts of self-destruction. Over the years, they will enlarge to fissures. He had a passion when he was thirteen: he loved table tennis. He played for the Yorkie and represented the club in a Liverpool tournament. In a final match, he'd been playing a boy from Blackpool. As they were changing sides, the boy had tapped Trenchy's ankle; Trenchy battered him and was expelled from the tournament. He never played the game again. He gave up his training runs in the cathedral grounds, he gave up his daily two-hour practice session; he threw away his sponge-rubber bat, his sneakers, his sweatshirt, his tracksuit. It was throwing away a part of his life.

Trenchy was faintly aware of this trail of destruction and was unable to control it. He knew he should be studying for his C.S.E. instead of staring out of the window. Every boy in the classroom knew that. Some would never summon the intelligence to study; others, like Trenchy, wouldn't work. It wasn't ignorance of the laws of success that prevented them from studying. It was the weight of the tenements, the ghetto, the wound in their heads. Only one boy had ever left St Martin's to study for his O Levels, then for his A Levels, and finally gone on to Sheffield University to study physics. Joe Barnes, the headmaster, was very proud of this boy.

The majority sat through the years, shuffling their books as a blind man would cards, unable to see the words and figures inscribed in them. It wasn't their fault. When they looked down at their hands they saw they held abstracts–French and geography and history and physics–the smatterings of an archaic knowledge. Trenchy's favourite subject was woodwork, but it was only a subject. Shite, they'd been given tools which fitted no machine they'd ever see; so they stopped looking at them. The teachers knew this and they only went through the motions of teaching. The education they had to impart was only secondary, in name and quality, their job was to keep the boys occupied until they reached the age of sixteen. One day, Joe Barnes had a class to take, so he set an essay. He found the majority couldn't write the English language or read it. The machine has long since broken down, but since they have no other the teachers continue to tend it. It leaves little imprint on the metal of the boys' minds; neither shapes nor hones them. They pass through it unscathed, dropping out at the first convenient exit.

Trenchy only wanted to leave school to collect the reward of the pay-packet. All his life he had been accustomed to a system of reward and punishment. Dependent on the passing or failing of exams. Primary school, secondary school, O Levels, A Levels, university. Each failure is for him a stark landmark, whereas the reward for leaving school is money. He has been told that the world is waiting to employ him, to reward him for his labours with a wage-packet that will buy him all his immediate dreams. Gear, beer, beef, a motor. Sitting in the schoolroom the choice afforded by a pay-packet seems to Trenchy dazzling and infinite. A rainbow that will begin the moment schooldays are over . . .

PROBATION OFFICER: *'While they're in school they're constantly promised the better life. They're told industry is waiting for them with good jobs and good money. They expect so much when they leave school. In Liverpool there are no jobs, or else very badly paid ones.'*

. . . only to blacken and shrivel the moment he starts the journey.

As he stared out of the window, Trenchy had an idea. If they weren't going to change the schools, he should be paid to stay in. Not just 50p. That would be when he was five. It would increase as he grew older: an extra week's wage for passing, time and a half for homework done, double time for excellent work, incentives and bonuses for passing exams. At sixteen, he would be getting the same as industry was paying, at eighteen with A Levels twenty sheets a week. That would keep him in school, studying, as long as possible. Those who were too stupid would just shift into a factory. At the moment Trenchy received one pound a week pocket money, and that was twice as much as most of the other boys.

The school bell sounded, like a fire alarm, and in a moment the classroom was empty. Trenchy drifted down the corridor with Devo and Beno and Mac. They all belonged to the Yorkie and sometimes also to the Park Road Boot Boys. Membership in the gang depended on one's own whim. If you lived in the area you were part of it, if you wanted to be.

Trenchy paid lip-service to the gang. Being a part of them meant trouble and, because of this, when they reached the yard he drifted away. There were a few black boys in the school and they stuck protectively together. Most of them would have preferred Paddington Comprehensive where their spars were.

Trenchy picked himself a spot near the gate and leant against the wall. The sun was warm and he closed his eyes drowsily; there were five minutes to wait for dinner. He opened them quickly when he heard boys running towards him. Beno was in front of the small crowd.

'There's Marko,' he shouted.

Marko was on his way down to Duff Gardens. He took a puff on his joint and calmly blew the smoke out at the kids.

'You fuckin' nigger,' Beno shouted. 'We'll batter you one day.'

'Yah,' Marko said. 'Why don't you do it now, you honky bastard.'

'We'll fuckin' kill,' Mac screamed.

'Not before I fuckin' tear your balls off.'

Beno found a stone, took a run and threw it at Marko. Marko sensed it. It seemed he could see their movements through his back. He sidestepped and the stone bounced and hit the wall. His headache had returned. The pain would increase as he moved down the sloping streets.

Marko laughed. Fuck the honkies. He had a pocketful of money. The finger from Social Security had come around at 12.30 and paid him twelve sheets and change. Marko'd immediately gone to pick up Ato.

'I got no money la,' Ato said mournfully. 'You go by yourself. I'll buy my drag this evening.'

'I'll buy it now; you do it in the evening. C'mon.'

Ato threw down his brush and ran out of the Jones. They first visited the Prince's Park pub to look for Tony. He always had a good supply of drag and was their regular connection. He wasn't there. They trotted to the Alex. It was so warm that they both yearned to have a long, calm smoke lying out on the grass. Tony was in the Alex, sitting on the bench next to the juke box. He was a small, pale, almost Arab-featured man. He looked as if he was on the hard stuff: his nostrils always seemed to quiver nervously. There were a dozen other men in the pub, who after a quick glance at Marko and Ato returned to their joints. Tony sold Marko a small lump, about half the size of a sugar cube, for 50p. Marko smelt and expertly felt its texture. It looked good. He and Ato crossed to Carter Street and settled themselves on the railings that ran round the play area. It was a small, oval patch of grass littered with concrete slides, unimaginative lumps, balls and hollows. No child ever played there. Marko broke the lump in half and gave Ato his share. After a moment's hesitation Ato brought his half next to Marko's. They were near-exact in size. Because of the breeze, they helped each other to make and roll their joints. They lit up and sucked in a deep lungful of smoke.

Two children were crossing the grass with a white woman. Marko exhaled.

'Hey, you seen Alan la,' he called to the children.

'He's still in bed,' the woman replied.

'I didn't ask you, you white cunt,' Marko shouted angrily. 'I asked the kids.'

'Fuck off, you black bastard.'

'Honky cunt.'

They shouted obscenities at each other until the woman turned the corner. Marko hated white pussy. One evening in Rank's dance-hall this pretty white pussy came up to him and said, 'Haven't we met before?' Marko groaned; what an old line. 'Fuck off,' he said. 'Why?' she asked. Marko felt physically sick. He called a half-caste girl and told her to get rid of the white cunt before he threw up.

Ato began to laugh.

'What are you laughing at?' Marko demanded. 'That's a real evil woman la, I'm telling you.'

'I know la, I know. I just felt like it.' He wasn't sure why he'd laughed; it was probably a surge of joy as the drag began to take effect.

Marko jumped off the fence and stretched lazily.

'I'm going home. You coming?'

'Naw, I'll go home too.'

They parted, puffing their joints. Marko stopped at a block of three-storey council-flats in Windsor Street. It was a hundred yards away from St Martin's.

'Alan,' he shouted. A sleepy black head eventually looked out of the top-floor window. 'I'll be back in ten minutes.' The head nodded and withdrew.

Another stone skipped and bounced past Marko. The nape of his neck was raw with nerves as he moved out of range from the school. There'd be others watching and waiting. He passed them, bunched in twos and threes, sitting on steps, leaning against walls, stopping their rap to watch him pass. They'd call to him when he'd safely passed; loud obscenities that threatened future pain.

Marko reached Duff Gardens and ran up the stairs. He stopped for only five minutes in the flat. He first handed five pounds to his aunt for rent and food. It was his Friday lunchtime routine whenever he had a job. A pound and change he pocketed; five pounds he placed in a tin box under his mattress. There was never much in it no matter how hard he tried to save. Last year he'd managed to put aside forty sheets, but his aunt had fallen ill and he'd spent all the money taking her medicines and presents in hospital. It had all gone in eight days.

Ato was exhausted by the time he reached home. It was a half-hour walk down Prince's Road and along the park rails to Cairns Street: he lived on one of the outer borders of the ghetto. When he saw the house with its peeling paint, his depression returned. Inside all was silent. The workshop had closed for lunch and his flat was empty. His depression returned as he drifted restlessly through the four rooms. He looked up at the ceiling and shuddered, and kept his head bowed as he warmed his dinner. It was a meat stew. His mother, Annie, had cooked it the previous day and she always made enough to last two or three days. It saved her cooking; not that she did much of it. The children usually made their own food from the shopping she dropped in a cupboard by the stove. Their regular diet was egg, sausage, toast and beans. Ato sat on the edge of the sofa and ate quickly. The kitchen/living-room/launderette needed an airing. And cleaning. Cigarette butts were scattered on the faded carpet and ash formed a grey film over the plastic sofa and the linoleum floor. The room reeked with the pungent smell of detergents and spices. Washing-powder had the stronger odour.

He dropped the empty plate in the sink. The itch had begun and he scraped angrily at his wrist. Though he was frightened, he forced himself up the stairs, compelled to confront a thing that made him physically sick. He hesitated on the landing outside the upstairs flat, carefully examined the floor and the door before pushing it open with his foot. Cautiously he entered. The furniture was well worn and thickly covered with dust. The dust danced in the sunlight. The paperback was lying where he'd dropped it in the morning. He touched it with his toe and jumped back as if it would bite. With his fingertips he picked up the book and slowly, very slowly, holding it as far from his body as possible, he opened it. They were still there. In fright and disgust he hurled the book across the room. Thousands of lice, resembling black dust, scattered on to the floor.

Ato turned and ran from the room. Like most of the poor he has an inherent fear of lice and personal dirt. These two are the accepted visible symbols of his poverty. When the middle class and the rich look at him, the first accusation that will be levelled at him is that he is dirty and lice-ridden. Dirt is the universal term of denigration. The rich think the poor are dirty and, ironically, the poor believe the rich are dirty. Marko once stood next to a wealthy councillor, and the sight of a dark mark on the man's neck fulfilled all his worst fears, the rich never bathe. The white believe the black dirty, the black the white. Dirt is a convenient, identifiable disease which can be wished on anyone.

What frightens Ato as he runs down the stairs is not the sight of those little insects. It is the sudden visible proof that the rich, the middle class, all his enemies who have at some time or the other called him dirty, are right. He is dirty. For so many years he has tried to keep himself protected and intact, like a crouching boxer, until he suddenly looks up and is hit very hard. He is about to sink to his knees and fold. Ato can confide in no one except his family. The fear of contamination, of becoming another dirty poor man, would be too much for his spars.

Ato can only eliminate one of his worries. He must have a bath, scour his skin clean, regain some of his lost protection. Almost frantically, he starts to strip. The bathroom is half a floor down, and he runs the water from the geyser so hot that he nearly faints when he gets into the tub. He knows, however, that it's doing him good. The pores are being cleansed, the dirt is floating free of his body.

When he returned to the flat, his skin pink with scrubbing and perfumed with soap, his mother was in the kitchen.

'They're still up there,' Ato announced. 'What are we going to do?'

'I went to Housing and they promised to send an inspector.'

'Ten fucking years we've been asking to move and they're going to send an inspector. I can't take it. If we don't move in the next week, I'm going to go mad. I can feel it.'

His mother was quiet. She too was depressed by the lice. She was normally a good-natured, happy-go-lucky woman. She was in her late thirties, early forties, and pleasantly plump. In later years, booze would bloat her body and blotch her white skin, but now she was still pretty and lazily sensual under the surface puffiness of a late night. Her red hair lent her a visual vivaciousness.

Annie had been born on Merseyside and spent her early years in orphanages, until she was adopted by foster parents. She'd left school very early to work, and when the time came, she married a black man. She'd always admired them. As a girl she'd see them on the trams and buses and wanted to meet them. She remembers on one tram journey a big fat black man who picked her up and bounced her on his knees and gave her a sweet. She had married a Trinidadian called Atkinson and had been widowed ten years. He had been killed on the M4, when his car jumped the central barriers during a police chase. Annie preferred the black people and the Toxteth ghetto to her own people and culture. When her husband died she could have moved away but she'd decided to spend her life with black people. They had a greater zest for living than white people. Parties, shebeens, boat cruises on the Mersey, sudden darting visits across the country to another ghetto for a party, the drinking, the laughing, the good sex. She never hid her sex life from her children. Ato knew most of her lovers; her room was directly opposite his. Sometimes they'd leave her money; at other times gifts that had fallen off the backs of lorries.

Earlier in the year one of her lovers had taken her to his country, Nigeria, for a two-month holiday. The children stayed with her sister in Wales. It was her first visit abroad and Annie had loved Nigeria. The people had excited her, and the heat, and she'd spent all her time not with the expatriate English lounging around the posh social clubs in Lagos, but with the black people in those noisy drinking-bars which were one glorious, unending shebeen. The

visit had widened her horizons and when she returned she talked
constantly about what she'd seen.

'If you'd been born and brought up in Nigeria, you wouldn't be
having such an easy life,' she'd tell the children. 'You'd be working
from morning to night. I saw children of four and five working for
a living. Hard, physical work, not some easy job.'

None of them listened.

'If you'd been living in Nigeria,' she'd tell them, 'you'd obey me
bloody quick. All the children obey their parents. If they don't,
they'll get a bloody thick ear, I'm telling you.'

It didn't make them obey her any the more.

The relationship between Annie and her children was more that
of an older friend than of a mother. She was too good-natured and
self-centred to play the role of parent. She never tried to rule them;
only to act as their adviser. For instance, she advised Ato and his
spars not to pressure the pigs. The pigs can play a lot rougher than
you kids, she'd say. And they did. As a flat-mate she seldom pulled
her weight. Her daughters complained she never cleaned up, that
they had to cook, that they had to do the laundry. Annie never had
the time. She'd get up at ten and by eleven she was out of the flat,
returning late at night. However, she did care enough for the
children to worry about them. She worried when Ato spent a year
in an approved school in north Wales. She would try to visit him
every weekend, and when he was released she advised him to take
the catering course at Liverpool College and enrol as a ship's cook.
She knew he wasn't capable of anything else.

'All I can do for you, John,' she'd tell him, 'is give you advice. It's
up to you to take it or leave it. I can't force you to do anything.'

It wasn't her fault she couldn't do more. She herself had never
inherited anything other than advice. She had the accumulated
wisdom of surviving as best she could, and having the good times
when she could. If her husband hadn't died, she knew he would
have abandoned her for a younger woman at some time in their
life. She was philosophical about this fate which could have befallen
her; she saw it in all the other mixed marriages. The ghetto seemed
at times almost totally populated by lone women looking after
children, whose husbands had returned 'home', or moved to
another woman. Annie understood the man's urge now that she'd
been to Nigeria. There each man had several wives. The black man
was used to another way of life and Annie could see no reason why

he should abandon it and be monogamous for his white woman's sake.

Annie was careless with her life, shifting it forwards to old age in leaps and bounds; she taught her children to live the same way. It was all good experience, she would say, for the children to grow up in a tough ghetto. Once you'd learnt to survive here, you could survive in any jungle.

'But did you *go* to the Housing Department?' Ato persisted.

His mother demurred. 'I rang them. I just didn't have time, John. I promise I'll make it tomorrow.'

'You've been saying that for ten years,' he said. He wasn't accusing her of neglect. He was all too aware that a person could be busy without doing anything.

'I know,' his mother said. 'But we do have our application in for a council house. The fucking trouble is that you've got to see them every day before they'll do anything.'

The Atkinsons were in every respect eligible for a council house. She was a widow; she had four children; and they lived in a sub-standard house.

The Atkinsons are only one of hundreds of families wanting to move—from old houses to council houses, from big houses to small ones, from small ones to big ones, from one estate to another. The pressure on the Housing Department is enormous. However, the whole problem has been aggravated by a bad decision made by the city planners years ago. They'd decided to run a motorway through the two adjoining territories in conjunction with a slum-clearance scheme. The proposed route cut a wide swathe through densely populated areas on its way to join up with Park Road from Smithdown Road. Houses, pubs, shops, cafés, launderettes, betting parlours were wiped out. The incomplete devastation has left mounds of rubble, waste ground, half-demolished houses. By the time the motorway was abandoned it had displaced hundreds of families and wiped out a community. Unsure what to do next after this bout of destruction, the planners have done nothing. The renovation of the old houses has stopped; the new council-house programme moves forward jerkily. A block here, a block there, like some mad giant tumbling bricks about.

To the people who live under its erratic shadow, the Department is a giant; a monolith on which they can inflict no wounds, for which they cannot find any controls, nor receive redress for their grievances.

BANK MANAGER: *'Economically, the whole area is running down. The Planning Department is partly to blame. They've knocked down a number*

40

of houses and services, and people have been moved out. The shops on Great George Street are due to be demolished in two years. No one's got any idea what they're going to do next. We just wait. We can't attract new investors because your shop or firm can be demolished. Until something definite is planned no new investments will be made here. The docks closing has also affected us all.'

IAN SCHOLES, of the Liverpool Planning Department: *'We aren't sure what to do next. We now realise that planning can only be done after a complete study of the human problems involved. We had a study made last year. It's called the Social Malaise Report. It's supposed to be confidential. It tells us what the problems are but not quite what to do about them. We are so far away from Toxteth and that whole area; not only in distance but also mentally. We've no idea what it's really like living in those tenements with all that concrete and tarmac. Sure, we drive through on inspection tours and just see the surface. For instance, we're planning to close Windsor Street to through traffic. On paper it's a good idea. But now that we know about the fighting what effect will it have? Traffic could be a deterrent to the fighting. And also, by closing the road, we are psychologically isolating the black people. We're making it into an island ghetto. We are not trying to create a ghetto in Toxteth but we are unable to stop the process. Originally we were treating black and white as equals in the allocation of housing. But the whites all want to move out of the area and when we try to move others in they refuse to go. Black people don't want to move out, and those who have want to move back in. We can't force people to do things. Maybe we should weight the black people and treat them specially. You know what happened in 1972. . . .'*

That was a time of madness. It was the moment of dissolution of a long, silent marriage which suddenly revealed that the two partners had nursed a deep hatred of each other.

The fighting between black and white broke out on the Falkner Estate, where a new block of corporation houses had just been completed. Across the road from the block were the old tenements, crowded with poor white people. One day they looked across and there in those shining brand-new houses were the niggers. They'd expected that they would be the chosen ones.

One Friday night their frustration exploded. They lined up along the streets, men, women, kids, and hurled bricks and obscenities at the people who'd stolen their houses. The black people tumbled out of their homes, dressed in their night clothes. When they saw the white mob, they sent runners through the

41

streets of the ghetto to collect the black kids. Around fifty of them came; they were the Black Panther Party and the Black Panther Men. They answered the call, and they came dressed in their leather jackets. Falkner estate became a place of siege. The blacks set up barricades to keep the whites out, the kids patrolled the area at nights. It was a hot time. They were defending their country from assault. For three days they fought each other and the police.

It wasn't the physical side of the fighting that hurt. The wounds were inflicted by words and emotions. Both had lain dormant for so many years and now, when they spewed out, like acid they stung and scarred the combatants. The black man in Liverpool, conditioned for so long into believing himself an equal, had his eyes suddenly opened. It was as if the lids had been ripped off and now the eyes would forever remain wide open. He was black, alien and unwanted. The white, who in turn had been conditioned to believe himself racially tolerant, discovered an antagonism he never knew existed. Neither side has ever recovered. The names they called each other still haunt the present–honky, nigger–and they watch each other across the boundary walls their minds have created.

Annie had been offered a house down in the Dingle, but like other black families she didn't want to move out. Not with children who were milk brown in colour and had kinky hair.

4

THE skin on Mrs Bickley's face looks tight. It seems to be pulled back tensely over her broad forehead and around the corners of her mouth and eyes. The wrinkles are like her features, sharp. She is a brave woman for she is the mother of the Bickley boys. This is one cause for the worry in her face. She is ashamed of her sons. She hates them battling in the streets, and nothing depresses her more than to know that Dave is King of the Boot Boys.

Mrs Bickley was legendary among the fighters. In mid-battle, in utter darkness, she would wade through the two sides, miraculously unharmed by the bricks and bottles, to slap and grab her two younger sons. The elder ones she could never catch. She wouldn't have minded if they fought the Boot Boys from the Dingle. What she hated was that they fought the coloured boys. 'I've slapped them, their father's belted them, but they still keep fighting the coloureds,' Mrs Bickley would tell her friend, Mary. Mary was her best friend and visited her every day at around eleven for a cup of tea. She'd used to live in James House but she'd been lucky and managed to have herself moved to the Dingle.

The four-roomed flat the Bickleys lived in was tiny for the size of the family. All the rooms were packed with furniture and the front room, with its chaos of chairs and sofas, looked like a furniture store. With nine children to look after, and a husband, Mrs Bickley had her hands full.

The eldest of her children, Maureen, was her favourite. Maureen was different from the others. She was a serious girl and held herself aloof from the other children and the tenement life. She had a good secretarial job in the city and she'd spent her holidays in Torremolinos with her office friends. She was the only one in the family who'd ever been abroad. Mrs Bickley would threaten all her other children with death if any of them pulled Maureen into the gang troubles. She was frightened for Maureen.

43

Being a Bickley was enough to get yourself battered by the coloureds or the Dingle gang. The second girl, June, had been battered by the coloureds immediately outside James House. She was partly to blame as she used to hang around with Dave and his spars. The battering had maimed June in spirit; she seldom left the flat and spent nearly all day sitting in a dazed dream by the television set. If the boys, Dave, Harry, Jimmy or Al, were hurt in the fighting, Mrs Bickley no longer cared. When Dave came back with his cut cheek she said, 'I told you so.' When eleven-year-old Jimmy returned from hospital with wounds in his scalp she said, 'I told you so.' She was too exhausted spiritually to do more.

Mrs Bickley was a good, traditional working-class woman. She accepted her role fatalistically. She was the womb for her husband's semen, the cook for his mouth, the rearer of his children. Neither she nor the children saw much of him. All the years he'd been a docker, he'd leave for work in the morning, return for tea at six, read the papers and spend the rest of the evening down in the pub.

He'd had vast respect in those days when he was a docker. He was a mythological figure not only to his family but to his friends and neighbours and to society. The myth was built on his physical strength, his stubbornness; he belonged in part to the land, in part to the sea, and he was opinionated, with a powerful command of crude English language. He could fight and swagger and drink. He worked hard for high wages and could, if he wished, hold an island country to ransom. The myth was reinforced by the fact that dockers are a closed society; like kings they pass on their lucrative office to their sons, and the sons to their sons. The job was a sinecure for which the only qualification necessary was to have a father for a docker. It was a territory, a kingdom he guarded jealously. It gave him and his family an arrogance and a pride which made them superior to many of their neighbours. His son was granted the same dignity and he knew when the time came he would wear the mantle of his father.

The end to Mr Bickley, a broad-shouldered, slightly stooping man, came coldly and quickly. He should have expected it, but like all men he didn't believe his life had an end. He was made redundant. It was an ignominious end. The blustering, swaggering idol didn't shatter; it dissolved.

Sometimes he wanders down to those deserted docks. Those that are now empty should look desolate and destroyed, yet they only look as if everyone had gone off on holiday and would quite soon be back. At any moment the cranes might start to rumble, the ships' sirens echo across the Mersey, the whine of the fork lift trucks pick up and men be seen cursing and shouting above the din of machinery. In the empty warehouses, he would stand like a wounded animal, his head lifted to catch the faint shifting odours. Oil, metal, bananas, coffee. . . . They were becoming weaker. Soon the large warehouse would smell only of musty, stale dust. Further up the Mersey some of the docks were still working. The ships that came were few now. The wake would remain long after they'd passed, undisturbed by the passage of another vessel, the froth licking the piers lazily and weakly.

Mr Bickley was destroyed. Coldly and abruptly he had been drained of his dignity, his pride, his capacity to be a man. He had been a docker and so unlike other men. He hadn't worked on a factory floor, caged in by a roof, machines and noise, or in an office. He was a docker, and redundancy removed the glitter and status not only from his own life but also from that of his family. In the eyes of his wife, his children, his friends, his neighbours, he had become stateless. He had shrunk down to the ordinary and, worse, he was now unemployed in a city where jobs were hard to find. On his redundancy pay he took the whole family to a Butlin's in Wales for a week. It was a defiant gesture in keeping with the romance of his old job. There was no joy in it for him, though the children loved every minute of the holiday. It was the best time they'd ever had in their whole life–one week at Butlin's.

When he returned from the holiday, he had to face reality. He was in his late forties with long, bleak years ahead of him. He didn't want the dole, but he took it for a while, and then decided to become self-employed. It wasn't much of a job. Each week he travelled to Manchester to buy cheap clothes wholesale, and brought them back to sell to the tenement families. It could never be the same as being a docker: he knew that from the way the boys treated him. He'd shrunk and lost his old authority. He could thrash them with his worn black belt but they no longer listened. They took the beating stoically and repeated the offence. They blamed him for having lost them their precious inheritance. There was no longer a mantle to be worn. They had to look for work like other boys in school.

From 12.30 on, like pins drawn to a magnet, the children began to return home–Harry from his laundry job, Dave from Smith's, the others from school or play. The moment of silence was shattered as each demanded his food. The boys were the worst. They held to the tradition that the woman was there to feed them and to be on hand when needed. Dave always had baked beans, toast and sausages. If his mother varied the diet, he would cook the food himself and sulk. As usual Mary was visiting and Mrs Bickley was continually reminded how nice it was in the Dingle in a council house rather than a flat.

'I wish they'd give us a house in the Dingle,' Mrs Bickley said. 'This place drives me mad; there's no room to even breathe sometimes. Every day I'm down at the Housing Department; every day they say, "We'll look into it." Bloody bastards. You'd think with nine children they'd do something.'

'I don't want to move to the Dingle,' Dave said.

'And I know why. One of these days you'll get yourself battered by those Dingle boys. And I won't lift a finger to help you. I don't know why you fight the coloureds now. In school a lot of my friends were coloured–I know I don't have any colour prejudice.' Mrs Bickley shook her head for the thousandth time. 'I wish you were both thieves rather than fight the coloureds.' It was a gesture to her illusions. Mrs Bickley knew her sons stole but she hated to admit it to herself and granted them innocence. 'You keep on fighting, what do you think will happen?'

'Nothing,' Dave said and swaggered to the mirror above the fireplace to admire himself. He thought himself very handsome and often dreamed of being a film star.

'You're very brave as long as you're here, aren't you?' Mrs Bickley said. 'I hope they catch you one day and teach you a lesson you'll never forget.'

'They won't catch me,' Dave laughed. 'I'm too clever for them.'

His mother snorted in disgust. She never won an argument with Dave, for like her he was stubborn. Dave finished his dinner and, after preening himself a bit longer in front of the mirror, grabbed his jacket and ran out. He usually spent half an hour of the dinner break at the Yorkie.

The Yorkie's faded red door was badly scarred. The wood had been savagely gouged by knives, steel bars and boots. In some places it was almost white with wounds. On the door was Billy, a plump, sad-looking young man with shoulder-length hair, who always looked scruffy and half-asleep. He represented an experiment by the Settlement, and was a human showpiece: he was an ex-Borstal boy. The Yorkie was run completely by reformed boys from the neighbourhood. Billy's one bright deed, which he frequently boasts of, was that he'd been gripped by the pigs screwing the old cathedral.

'Chas in?' Dave asked and tried to slip past. Billy stuck out his hand. It cost 5p to get in.

'I got no money la,' Dave said. 'I'll owe it to you this evening after I get me pay. Promise.'

'In the billiard room,' Billy said and allowed Dave in. Billy was bored and feeling tired. He wished he could be lying in his room listening to sounds.

The interior of the Yorkie is bleak and ugly. The concrete floors are cold and bare, where the walls are unmarked by felt-penned graffiti, they are chipped and cracked. The paint is a sickly, faded red and yellow. It's a sad place, like the inside of a prison, and smells of decay and urine. The walls and furnishings are only punchbags for those who find themselves trapped inside. There is no grace or warmth to the interior of the Yorkie. It reflects only the exterior landscape of tenements and captures the same feeling of desolation. The kids treat it as they do their world outside; brutally and uncaringly.

The Yorkie has three levels. Half a stairway below the entrance is the disco. It looks the most attractive room because it's always in darkness and overcrowded, and the walls are bright with dayglo paint that shimmers like rich mirages in the fluorescent light. Above that are the recreation rooms. The large central hall looks deserted with two table-football machines and a coffee counter. On one side of the hall is the T.V. room, which is always a wreck, the sofas and chairs disembowelled and broken, the television under continuous repair. On the other side is the billiard room. This is the domain of the older boys and they guard their preserve jealously. The door is always jammed shut and any beef or younger boy who enters is immediately chased out. Its walls too are bare. Most of the graffiti declare: Bicklo is King. The billiard table is scarred with knife slashes and the cushions sag like loose slingshot. The cue's broken and the balls are cracked. The game is played non-stop. Next to the billiard room is the table-tennis room. The tables have been repaired and broken countless times, until the Settlement has finally given up. The floor above is a large gym with a football 'pitch'. It's the least damaged because there's nothing to destroy. Leading off the gym is a small room piled high with old mattresses. It's a retreat for the older boys when the Yorkie is closed. It has the same magic as a secret, bushy dell on a vast private estate where the young can escape and play their private games.

Chas was in the billiard room watching Pat and Snowy playing snooker. Chas couldn't play because his right hand was heavily bandaged. Two weeks ago a slate thrown in the battling had cut the muscles. He couldn't move his two middle fingers. Chas was slim, and the weight of his upper body rested visibly on jutting hips which slid down to a non-existent bottom and thin legs. He could have been called a handsome boy, but his mouth was a thin split in his face; his blue eyes were cold, flat tunnels boring into the void.

Because of his hand, Chas was off work and flat broke. He'd given up battling permanently, though not thieving. His abstinence from fighting was imposed on him by the Law. If he was caught with a knife or a brick in his hand, they were going to send him away for a long time.

Chas was proud that he had been pronounced mad. Like an actor with his favourite review, he would often quote the words of the magistrate at his last court appearance. 'He called me a maniac and said I was a menace to the public.' Chas loved those words. The magistrate's opinion was based on Chas's having slashed a copper's face.

He and Bicklo had been out mugging one night. They usually concentrated on the Chinks down around Great George Square. The Chinks were small, and one boot in the head was enough. Chas, however, preferred to carry a small bar up his sleeve. They found a Chink walking alone up Kent Street at eleven and Chas had crept up behind him and brought the bar down hard on the Chink's head. Splat. He tore the scalp open, and for good measure he and Bicklo put the boot in. They were just lifting the Chink's money when the pigs turned the corner. Chas and Bicklo split, and the pigs lost Bicklo in the tenements. Three of them kept on Chas. He ran into Kent Gardens and found himself trapped on the top floor by one of the pigs. The pig was six steps below him with his truncheon out. Chas took off his heavy belt and swung the buckle end at the pig. The metal ripped the man's cheek from eye to mouth. The pig fell. Chas laughed. He kicked the pig in the ribs and bounded down the stairs. As he ran out of the exit the two pigs waiting on either side grabbed him by each arm. 'Got you, you fucking bastard,' one said and slammed his truncheon into Chas's side. Chas kicked the other pig before they slammed him into the back of the Rover. They battered him mercilessly on the ride back to the police station with the wounded pig. The Chink had eighteen stitches put into his head, the pig seven, and Chas was fined eighty pounds.

Chas was well known to the cops for 'affray', 'grievous bodily harm', 'taking and driving', 'breaking and entering' and every other small crime common to the kids. They were waiting for Chas. If they saw him walking down the street, even with his beef, they'd stop and search him. Once he'd managed to drop his flick knife, seconds before they reached him. That was close. The cops would have loved to have him for carrying an offensive weapon.

'You ready?' Chas asked when Dave entered. Bicklo nodded and they moved to the door.

'Where you goin' la?' Snowy asked. 'I'm comin'.'

'Later,' Chas said coldly. 'Later la.'

They turned right outside the Yorkie and slowly climbed the slope towards the old cathedral. They didn't talk. Both pulled nervously on their cigarettes and every few yards turned to look back. No one was following or watching them. They tried to swagger but it was difficult climbing a steep street and swaggering as well. Thirty yards before they reached St James's Road, they took one last careful look around and then quickly ducked into one of the derelict buildings. It was gloomy and treacherous inside. The house smelt of damp rotting wood and paper and urine. It was a suffocating smell. They picked their way carefully through the house. Beams and masonry lay on the floor which in places didn't exist at all. A deeper blackness would suddenly reveal the basement. They emerged into a narrow yard and shuffled parallel to St James's Road until they reached a well-preserved wall. They peered over the top.

'You sure no one's in?' Bicklo whispered.

'Course,' Chas said. 'I sussed it out ten minutes ago. They went out in their motor.'

Bicklo still hesitated. Chas gripped the top of the wall, found a niche for his boot and pulled himself up. He dropped down the other side. Bicklo followed. They found themselves in a small, well-kept yard and crossed it to peer into the kitchen. It was empty. Chas took a step back and kicked at the door lock with the heel of his heavy shoe. It took three kicks before the wood splintered and broke. They were inside. The kitchen was quiet and clean. Chas moved quickly to the front door and bolted it. He didn't want the owners to walk in unannounced. They listened to the silence of the house. Outside a car accelerated past. They felt powerful. It was theirs for a few minutes, to do what they wanted with. It was a small, neat house. The walls were divided by heavy wood beams, the horse brasses and candlesticks glittered, and the stairs were narrow. Bicklo ran up to the bedroom. He stripped the pillows of their covers and pulled open the dressers and threw open the cupboard. He hurled the contents of both on to the floor. The only object of value was a silver-backed hairbrush. He dropped it into the pillowcase and went downstairs. Chas had gathered together as much of the brass as he thought the pillowcase would hold. They filled it with plates, candlesticks and a transistor radio, working faster and faster. Most of the brass in the living-room was too big or heavy for the pillowcases and they threw it aside. Finally, the two pillowcases were full and, looking regretfully at the spoils they'd had to abandon, they retreated to the kitchen. Chas was hungry. He looked into the fridge. There was a piece of cold chicken and he stuffed it into his mouth. He washed this down with half a bottle of cold milk. He grinned at Bicklo and dropped the bottle on the floor. The milk spilt in a wide, jagged arc. Bicklo grabbed four eggs from the tray and dropped them into the spilt milk. Chas added ketchup and Bicklo a bag of flour. The pattern was ugly.

They returned to Nile Street the way they'd come. Chas stuck his head out first. There was no one to be seen in St James's Road; and below the only sign of life was outside the Yorkie. They ran down the slope, the pillowcases banging and clanging against their legs.

'How much you think we get for this stuff?' Bicklo asked. They were back in the billiard room after hiding the two pillowcases in one of the empty buildings near the Yorkie.

'Fiver,' Chas said after deep thought. To both it was an adequate amount of money, although what they'd stolen was worth at least fifty pounds. One of their problems was that neither of them knew of anyone who'd give them more than a fiver for anything. So they always expected a fiver, whatever they stole.

'Later,' Bicklo said and jogged out of the Yorkie. He glanced up to St James's Road, there was no one around, and he hurried down the street to Smiths.

When Chas sauntered out of the Yorkie half an hour later there were two police cars parked at the top of the road. He sat down on the steps and watched the cops with an amused smile. They'd found the mode of entry and three cops were entering the derelict house. Chas stopped smiling.

'Shite,' he swore. They'd forgotten the gas meter. He'd just have to screw the house again.

5

On his way back to work, Marko avoided passing St Martin's. He came up Hill Street to Windsor Street. He was feeling languid and didn't want any pressure from those honky kids.

'Alan!' Marko shouted as he reached the block of flats. Alan stuck his head out. 'Just eating la,' he shouted back.

Marko sat on the steps to wait and began to hum to himself. The hum gradually became a song, softly sung. He was remembering a time when he was very happy. This was before his friends broke up three years ago. Some of the black kids had formed a small pop group and Marko had been their bongo-player. It had been boss, really boss. The first concert the group had given, with Marko dressed in a black shirt, black trousers and black shoes, had been at the Lewis hall. The equipment hadn't been good, they were very nervous and the crowd sparse. But it had been cool standing up on the stage in front of people. The next gig had been at the Masonic pub. It had been another one-nighter. This time the sound system was good and the group confident. Marko knew this was what he was going to do all his life. The group were building up to a peak. At a charity youth evening they performed in the Philharmonic Hall. The Phil! A real stage, a real theatre, real dressing-rooms, a fantastic sound system. Every seat in the hall had been taken. For that night the group had all worn Afro shirts–white with black along the edges and around the neck–and Marko had worn black trousers. He'd felt sick as he'd walked out on to the stage. The crowd stretched back, row upon row, as far as he could see. He played with all his guts and all in a daze. When they finished the crowd exploded. They clapped and screamed and clapped and whistled. The sound drowned him; he was loved and wanted; he wished he could have stored it, like water in a tub, and immersed himself continuously in it. Backstage, after the show, the teeny boppers came for the autographs. It was as if they were the Beatles.

People touched them, talked to them. Marko saw one young beef nudge her mother desperately to ask her to get Marko's autograph, but the mother was too shy. It was boss la. Then his group began bickering with each other and he sold the bongos because he was broke. Finally, they split up. Marko would, at times when he was alone, still restlessly drum those rhythms. His eyes closed, he would recall the awesome applause. The hands beating together in praise of him. He couldn't believe it had all really happened. He would dream sometimes of turning back and recapturing it. But with each moment of life it slipped further and further away. It was too distant, and he couldn't summon the energy. Like everything else, once it had ended it ended forever. It was fading . . . fading. . . .

Alan nudged Marko to his feet and they wandered up to Berkeley Walk. Alan was playing truant from school. He had a year to go and hated every minute of it, and as it was Friday he'd decided to stay away. He had hoped it was going to be a good day, but it had begun real evil. His nan had given him five pounds the previous evening to buy a pair of trousers, but when she saw he wasn't going to school she'd demanded it back. Alan had calculated three pounds for the trousers and two for his pocket. In his rage at being lectured by his nan he'd thrown the money back.

Alan was short and stocky and black. He walked C-shaped. Head and hips stuck out while his arms hung loose. Alan, everyone knew, was a troublemaker. He was a gossip and a hustler and desperately trying to emulate his older brother, Sean, who was doing two years' Borstal for robbery. Alan's ambition to prove himself Sean's equal often got him into trouble. Last year the big boys had nearly wiped him out. Alan knew everyone in the ghetto, including the big boys who hung round the Alex, and as he was going his rounds, gossiping, hustling, running messages, he sometimes forgot who he was talking to. By accident he spread the word about a big robbery, and the boys nearly beat the shite out of him. These days he was Marko's *alter ego*. He was only taking the place of his brother, who'd been Marko's closest spar. Alan would egg Marko on to steal and fight.

There was little for either to do for the rest of the afternoon. The wallpapering had been finished by Jim, and only a door had to be painted. Marko allowed Jim to finish that as well. He lounged outside on the low parapet with a few spars. It was a warm afternoon, and he rapped lazily to Carlos and Kaye and Brian and Stan and Sausage.

'I won 10p yesterday,' Carlos boasted. Everyone wanted to know how, as it sounded like a new hustle. 'I raced Brian to that lamp-post there, and Leesup gave the winner 10p. Brian got five.'

'I could have beaten you,' Brian said and slyly looked around.

'Any bets?'

Nobody wanted to. Carlos was a good runner. Leesup, one of the big boys, had been taken, and it made everyone laugh.

'I'm getting pressure la,' Kaye said. 'Me mum goes on and on about my not working. Least three pounds of pressure she gives me everyday la. I keep telling her, why should I work. I get enough money from me dad.' His father owned a house in Granby Street and rented out the rooms. His mother lived in a council house and looked after the children.

'You're not gettin' as much pressure as Alan la,' Brian said with a grin. 'He's gettin' pure pressure from the beef I hear he's engaged to. You goin' to marry her, Alan la?'

Brian shot off the parapet as Alan lunged.

'I'm not gettin' engaged to any fuckin' beef,' he shouted. 'You watch it or I'll batter you. It's no joke la,' he added plaintively.

'Nothin' but pure pressure,' Brian chanted. 'You buyin' a house . . .' He ducked as Alan threw an empty coke-can and then ran after him. They disappeared round the corner.

Marko, bored, said, 'Later,' and sauntered up to Upper Stanhope Street. The boys had begun to talk about greasing their legs, faces and arms to ward off the grey, dull cracks that formed on the skin in the cold weather. It looked unsightly. The grease made the skin look rich and black and clear.

In Upper Stanhope Street, Marko saw Alan at the far end in front of the Monty Carlo chippy. He was talking to one of the big boys and then accompanied him to the gambling shop next to the post office. Marko smiled. Alan was hustling himself some money. He did it running. Borrowing 1p, 2p–whatever the particular person could afford to give–until he had enough. Sometimes he managed to get together 50p; on lucky days he'd make a whole sheet.

Marko suddenly spun on his heel and ducked into the shop. He leaned on the counter with his back to the window until he thought it safe to turn around. His mother hadn't seen him. She was looking the other way as she passed. He blew out in relief and ambled back to the street. On Parly he skirted the big man standing on the steps of the Rialto furniture store. . . .

Councillor Swainbank is a man in his mid-fifties. He'd taken a gamble by renting the long-empty Rialto cinema to store his furniture. The store is a jumble of old and new furniture, antiques, bric-a-brac. It caters mostly to the working-class man.

COUNCILLOR SWAINBANK: 'I've tried to get on with the coloured people in the area–my God, I've tried. It just doesn't work. Especially with those half-caste kids. They break into my place nearly every day now and steal something. Yesterday it was one dozen coffee tables. What on earth do they want with coffee tables? And you'd think someone would have seen them and reported it to the police. Not a word. They break in through the roof. They come across the roofs of the other buildings, kick in an upstairs window or smash the tiles and just drop in. I've thrown barbed wire round the rooftop, barricaded the windows, done everything. They still break in. I can't afford these losses. Look, I'm a working-class man, and I've sweated to get where I am. I fought for this country in the war; I've paid my taxes; I work long hours every day. All I see around me are layabouts, whom I'm supporting. They've got an easy life, I'm telling you.

'It's tragic. Toxteth has changed so much. I was born not more than half a mile from here. You wouldn't believe what it was like in those days. The houses were elegant, and you'd have carriages and those early motor cars moving slowly along Upper Parliament Street. Those houses are still good for a few number of years but for some reason they've let them rot. My mother was a skivvy in one of those grand houses. You know what a skivvy is? A servant girl. She'd work twelve hours a day, seven days a week, cleaning and polishing the mansion for half a crown a day and the left-over Sunday joint. Half a crown! The best part was the joint. It wasn't much but she'd wrap it up and bring it home on Mondays for us to eat. It was delicious. On Sundays, on Prince's Avenue, the nurses would take your young master and mistress for a stroll in their prams. Those big, high prams. And the girls would be dressed in black with white starched caps and bows. In the evenings, the master and mistress took their stroll down the avenue. There'd be quite a crowd there, and those open carriages would be drawn up and down. As a boy I used to see them every day. I was working even then. I had a small pushcart and I'd go around collecting old furniture which I'd sell.'

The change in Toxteth was gradual at first. As the rich moved out into the country, their houses were occupied by deans, professors and administrators, many of them people who worked for Liverpool University. They brought with them the solid values of the educated middle class, and those rich, gracious homes seemed to settle more comfortably into the earth as they moved in, to grow steadier and sturdy. The houses weren't neglected but there wasn't the money to maintain them in the style they were used to. The avenues still had their large, spreading trees and the small, square gardens, like Falkner Square, were neat and well tended. By the fifties, all this too began to change. The middle class, finding those large houses difficult to maintain, began to move into smaller, more comfortable homes that were being built for them in the suburbs. The landlords knew one family could no longer afford a house to itself, so they divided them into flats. Toxteth was no longer fashionable, and the poor began to move in. Soon the flats were turned into rooms for those who couldn't afford even that, and the new poor who took the rooms were the blacks.

Toxteth is the ward of Councillor Lady Simey. She's a contrast to the people she represents in the local government. She's a slim, energetic woman in her early sixties.
MARGARET SIMEY: *'It seemed to happen so suddenly. One year I was representing white, middle-class people, and when I turned round nearly half my constituents were black. It was a challenge to me and I was determined to represent my new constituents the best way I could. I was very lucky really. My husband and I had spent a year in Jamaica and we learnt so much of the people. I don't think I ever enjoyed a year more in my life. When I found there were black people in my ward, I was really delighted. They have so much more life in them . . . though I do admit there are a few trouble-makers as well. When my husband was alive, he used to adore the hybrid. In fact, I believe as well the hybrid is superior, physically and mentally. You've seen those really attractive children of mixed parents. I know most of the black people. I meet and talk to them whenever I can. I try to support them as much as possible. Whether it's for a community project or against the police.'*
Lady Simey's enthusiasm was tempered slightly by the Black Power movement. She strongly supported Bill Johns. Unfortunately he was caught by the police while travelling in a car with petrol bombs in the boot.

Marko's detour round Councillor Swainbank was instinctive. He was aware of the Councillor's opinion of his people. The back of Marko's hand rigidly caressed the Councillor's Jaguar parked against the pavement as he passed. He drifted down Parly. He wasn't headed in a particular direction. Days always seemed too long. They stretched each sunrise like another eternity to be filled.

When school finished for the day, Trenchy wondered what to do. The time he'd spent in the classroom, staring out of the window, had been chipped painfully out of his impatient flesh. He had thought there would be so much to do. The streets stretched out like a long, primrose path to freedom.

The streets were empty of diversions as he walked back to James House. He saw Harry standing at the entrance of the laundry and stopped to rap a moment before moving on. He thought of joining the other boys who were hurrying down to Great George Street. Beno, Snowy, Bill, Steve. . . . However, he knew once they reached the railings in Upper Pitt Street, they'd stop, end up sitting on the railings watching the passing traffic, watching the passing people. The time they consumed was not spent doing absolutely nothing; it was spent waiting. They never knew what they waited for. The Yorkie was closed till the evening. There were no cafés, chippies, launderettes to hang around; no drag to smoke. They were waiting for something to happen. A fight, a car or house to screw, a beef to fuck.

Trenchy dropped in home, hoping someone would be there. The flat was empty: his mother didn't return from work until five, and his father would come in much later, and after tea spend most of the evening in the pub. Trenchy made himself a coffee and watched the children playing out in the yard. The games were simple and played without toys. A dozen young girls formed a circle playing secrets. They whispered and giggled to each other. The boys were throwing stones at one of their number who stood against the wall. The boy dodged each stone at the last moment; one glanced his arm slightly, and he lost. Another boy took his place against the wall.

Trenchy saw Gerald crossing the yard and went out to meet him. Gerald was one of his countless cousins. Trenchy's mother, who'd been born in James House, and whose own mother still lived there on the third floor, had eleven brothers and sisters.

They wandered down Parly and up Great George Street. They passed the boys sitting on the railing. Trenchy decided to go into town. He stopped first at Mary McConnell's sweet and cigarette shop to buy a fruit-and-nut chocolate. Mary's was the only sweetshop in Great George Street until Duke Street, which was past the Blackie. On her side of Great George Street were two Organ-makers who had located their firms as near the old cathedral as possible, a grocery, a betting shop and three used-car salerooms. On the other side, the west, were rows of council houses. Mary's side was due for demolition in three years and neither she, nor the other firms, were sure what they were going to do.

Mary McConnell is a plump, amiable woman whose shop is used as a meeting-place for all her friends. There are chairs on either side of the counter for them to rest their feet. Mary McConnell's best friend is Mary Owens, and regularly the two spend a few evenings together in the pub. Mary Owens is plumper than her friend and older. Her mother was a friend of Mary McConnell's mother. She is in her early sixties and has spent all her life in the area, except for a brief period during the war when she and her mother were moved up Parly to avoid the bombing. She lives now in a council house opposite Mary McConnell's sweetshop.

MARY OWENS: *'It was a grand place to live in then. The class of people haven't changed like up on the hill where the rich used to live and now its all coloured. The dockers lived here in the old days as they do today. The streets ran the same way but instead of these jerry-built, that's what I call them, jerry-built council flats, there were small, tiny houses. They'd be back to back with outside privies. Oh, being poor was hard but it was enjoyable. We had a grand spirit of community in those days. People were always helping each other. If someone wasn't seen for a day, one of the neighbours would knock on the door and find out if the person was all right. Very often none of us had the money to pay the rent, and we'd help each other out. If we didn't have the money, we'd fight together. When the bailiffs came to throw out a tenant, the whole community would block off the streets so that the men wouldn't be able to get through. We'd only allow the priest to cross the barricades. Father, we'd say, you can always go in. Not like nowadays. For instance, there's a young woman who lives above my flat and I never see the girl from one week to the next. She may be dead, for all I know. Nobody cares any more. In the old days, your neighbours and friends worried about you. They'd share what little food they had, and if you were sick they'd sit by you. In the late twenties, when no one had any work, everyone helped each other. It was a grand place to live in then, it was. You could leave your doors open all day without having anything stolen. In fact people left notes for the gasman and milkman telling him where the money was, and he'd walk in and out of the house. Today, if you leave a window open you won't find your flat when you return. When the men were out of work, none of them loitered on the streets, like the kids do nowadays. If the police caught you loitering they'd fine you five shillings. Five shillings, when all you earned was two pounds a week. And there weren't any gangs in those days.*

58

Oh, yes, there was one. The Chen gang. It was run by two half-caste Chinese boys, and all the rest of the gang were white. But they didn't do much harm. We called them a gang because they were always together. As children, we'd all have to be in bed by eight. My mother'd call me in by seven-thirty, feed and wash me, and after saying my prayers I'd be put to bed. We had a lot of games to play when we were children. Kick-the-can was one I liked, and on the open ground near Park Road we'd play rounders. Boys and girls together. We'd run messages for a sweet, and once a week we had a bath under the cold tap. I remember my father would strip down to his trousers and bathe in cold water whatever the weather. I loved to watch him. There were all the coloureds living around here. Not in Toxteth, though. Toxteth then was the rich. The blacks were further down near the docks; the Chinese were in Paradise Street; the Malays in Albert Square. We played with their children when we were young, went to school with them; a lot of us married them. We didn't fight each other like today, black against white. I don't know where the kids learnt their prejudice. Not from us, I'm sure.

'It was a grand place to live in in those days.'

On the way into town Trenchy passed other kids moving purposelessly towards the triangle. The older Beno, Paddy, Kevin. The were in singles, in twos, in threes and like him just moving for the sake of it. To make oneself believe, however momentarily, that one was busy. Trenchy didn't want to join them, though each time he passed one of them they'd say, 'You comin'?' Trenchy'd shake his head and say he was running a message into town. If you went with them, you'd get into trouble. It would just happen, without any of them controlling the event that was building up. One of them would say, 'Let's go up the street', and in ones and twos, curious to see what would happen up the street, they'd set off. It could be the sight of a nigger or a car with its door unlocked or a flat with an open window. As if sucked in by the coming event they'd all be suddenly fighting or stealing. While it was happening, their identities merged into one single creation which, viewed from the outside, resembled a huge, many-limbed monster that destroyed and pillaged and hurt. It was a need to be part of something happening that robbed them of their identities at that moment. They wished that, when the time came to remember what they had done that day, they could remember how with Beno and Snowy and Dave they'd done it. Their memories were interknit, they were mentally connected by shared events. If not with Dave

59

then with Paddy. Like a complex puzzle, they all fell into one pattern recognisable to every outsider–passer-by, police, magistrate, newspaperman–as hooligans. Trenchy knew this happened, and he avoided drifting with them as much as possible. It wasn't an easy decision, if you lived in the area, went to the same school, spent your evenings in the same streets and in the same youth club.

'What's happened, Trenchy?' they'd say. 'You scared of trouble? You don't like us? You're not pussy, are you? You must be a coward.'

Sometimes the mocking would be good natured; more often it was vicious. They distrusted the uncommitted. They'd pressure Trenchy continuously and call him 'strange', hinting at his virility. The pressure would also come from within Trenchy, to want to become a part of a larger group, not only for companionship but also for protection. It didn't matter that he'd never stolen or taken part in the fighting regularly; the niggers would recognise him as a friend of Bicklo and chase him down the streets. Because he was an only child and continuously in conversation with older people, he was more mature than the other boys. His mother found it embarrassing that after a sex lecture at school he'd sit down as an adult and discuss the subjects with her, ask her questions straight out, not ducking and blushing as she did.

But because of his loneliness Trenchy was also a fantasist. He would tell people things that were not true at all. He told his headmaster, Joe Barnes, that his parents were divorced and that he was living with his nan. When Trenchy's mother visited Barnes he expressed regret, out of politeness, over her divorce, to Mrs Trench's surprise. At times, Trenchy's habit was irritating to his parents. He spread a story that they were about to move, that his father was a travelling salesman. It wasn't only Trenchy who fantasised. All the boys and girls did it. They weren't telling lies, though they were to social workers and probation officers who came from a stratum of society above them and called the kids all 'bloody liars': thus judging them not by the kids' standards but by their own standards, whereby any statement which wasn't fact was a lie. The fantasy was usually believed in. Each act of defiance, for instance, against the pigs, against society, was first exaggerated and then implicitly believed in. They built a world around them, with themselves as heroes and heroines, quite out of step with reality but very necessary, for they had no other means with which to survive daily.

6

MARKO, Ato and Alan were standing outside the Monty Carlo chippy sharing a smoke when the pigs stopped outside the Berkeley pub. The two men who climbed out of the unmarked car were dressed neatly in suits, yet within a few minutes of their stopping everyone knew the pigs were around. You didn't hear or see the whispering. The news seemed to reach telepathically to everyone standing around in the streets. Maybe they knew intuitively, like animals on a savannah suddenly stiffening to an odour in the breeze that warns of danger before the hunter has reached their horizon. Marko tucked his smoke into the hollow of his hand. One of the big boys passed his plastic bag full of hash–at least twenty pounds' worth–to Alan to hold and drifted a few yards away, from where he could keep an eye on the pigs and Alan. The pigs came out of the Berkeley and drove the few yards to the Prince's Park and stopped opposite Marko. If the two men felt the hostility to their presence, they didn't show it as they entered the pub. The hostility wasn't to be seen; there was no murmur of violence to be heard in the evening air. But if it could have been seen it would have looked like a vapour, dark and sulphurous, rising from each and every person on the streets or in the pubs. Like Marko and Ato and Alan, the men suddenly seemed to strut, their backs straight, their haunches raised as if ready for the fight that could come. Again the word came, without sound. Marko picked it up and passed it on, and within minutes it would be down at the Alex and further along, deeper into Toxteth. Up and down Granby Street, hurrying into homes, past closed and locked doors to reach the ears of men and women who would be interested in the presence of the pigs. The pigs were looking for the man who had battered the girl outside the Alex. They knew who it was, the word said, and were looking for a youngish, tall black man. The men hanging around outside the Prince's Park relaxed: the pigs,

61

that night, didn't affect them. Marko relit his smoke and took a deep drag as the pigs came out. They might smell the pungent smoke but they gave no sign. Every man's turn came; soon it would be Marko's.

The pigs drove up Carter Street to the Alex, and Alan handed back the hash reluctantly. To have held a small fortune and then have to give it back. But he knew it wouldn't be worth the pressure if he had disappeared with it.

'Let's go and watch the pigs,' Marko said.

Ato nodded glumly, and all three set off at a quick walk. Ato was still depressed over the lice. He took the joint from Marko and sucked deeply, hoping soon he would be able to forget and forget.

As they cut across the waste ground towards the Alex an old crone passed them.

'The pigs are out,' she laughed in a high voice. 'Careful.'

'I know, old woman,' Marko said.

The three boys stood outside the Alex with a small crowd of men. With the pigs inside, nobody was entering. The Alex had a tough reputation and in some respects resembled a private club. There were watchers posted at both doors nearly every evening and they would have seen and heard the pigs as if they were a herd of charging elephants before they'd even come out of the Berkeley. The pigs came and stood on the pavement. For a long time no one moved. It seemed the pigs were defying someone to start something. Then, with the slow movement of men who know they've cowed the opposition, they climbed into their car and drove off. They never found the man who battered the girl.

The three boys started back to Upper Stanhope Street. It was nearing seven-thirty and they were wondering what they should do.

'Let's go to the Blackie,' Ato said.

Marko didn't say anything. He pursed his lips and kept walking. At that moment he didn't have much else to do. There was nothing to screw and. . . . Finally he nodded, and the three cut across the back streets and headed for the Blackie.

There were two routes they could take to the Blackie. The first–and there was little difference in the lengths of the journey–was down Upper Parliament Street and up Great George Street, and passed through Bicklo's territory. The other formed the alternate sides of the square. They could cut straight up Hope Street, down Duke Street and on to Great George Street.

On the way down to the Blackie, when they went in small groups of twos and threes, everyone invariably took the Duke Street route. Marko, Ato and Alan were no different. Hope Street ran parallel to the vast enclave of the old cathedral. The street seemed to be parallel to the dome and from that height they could look down on the park where a year ago they had trained to be Black Panthers. Folklore has it that the well in the grounds of the cathedral has curative powers and that any man with sickness will be made whole. The grounds were nearly always empty.

The boys stopped to roll a joint. Alan acted as look-out while Ato and Marko pulled out their makings. Marko took the first puff and passed it on. Gradually the drug was beginning to take effect. A few more joints and they'd be floating over the street. They talked about it on the way down Duke Street, as if the euphoria was new and they were exploring it for the first time.

'You know,' Alan said, 'when I'm not on it I feel small. Nothing works la. I can't talk clever, I can't think clever. When I am on it, I feel good, real good. I can make people laugh with me; I know I'm talking well.'

'It's not that la,' Marko said and stopped. He spread out his arms. 'On a high you own the whole fucking world. Nobody can touch you la. You've got control of your whole life like it's in your fucking fist.'

'That's it la,' Ato said and laughed. 'You've got it. It's. . . .' He jumped high in the air. 'It's getting up there and staying there, instead of coming down again. You know when I'm on a high I can see so clearly, I can hear clearly. As if I can see through walls and people. Once when I took acid I went down to the Pun Club la. I was standing in the corner looking at all the people and laughing. I knew what everyone of them was thinking la. I could see who was afraid, who was brave, who was . . . mean . . . who was good. I saw some pure evil in there la. And pure good. People were like glass right in front of my eyes. I knew what they were thinking and feeling. It was frightening la. I got so scared, I shan't take acid again.'

No one was listening to him. They'd heard it all before. Not once, often. They told and retold each other every experience that had affected their brief lives. The boys were at the garrulous stage, but as time passed and they sucked more and more hungrily on their joints, rushing to escape into paradise, they'd become quieter.

By the time they reached the Blackie the joint was finished. They were feeling lighter already as they ran up the steps.

From the outside the Blackie looked abandoned. Apart from the blackened dome, its granite walls were streaked with grime and dirt. The railed fence was rusted, and grass grew between the cracks of the paving-stones. Its pillars were scrawled with the names of the boys and girls.

Inside, though, the Blackie is a marvellous place for children. Like an Aladdin's cave, it's full of different treasures which change from day to day. Disco, inflatable, basket-ball, adventure playground, video tapes, sewing classes, cookery, pottery, movies, pop concerts, stage shows. The variety is endless. The circus schedule is changed continuously to entertain a fickle audience; to hold them for one more day off the streets. There are only two floors to the Blackie: a large wooden floored hall, roped off into sections, and a smaller basement. In the smaller rooms behind the main building are the administrative offices.

The Blackie works so well because it is run by the middle class for the poor. Bill and Wendy Harp, and some of the youth workers are white middle class. They are helped in the running of the Blackie by some of the black people, but the administration and organisation are controlled by the Harps. Bill and Wendy and the other middle-class youth-workers have the disciplines of control, of success, of achievement inculcated into them. They came to work every day whether they felt like it or not; attended the planning conferences; fulfilled their share of the labour. However, no matter how much they succeeded in making the Blackie work, they couldn't get the kids to identify with them always. They came from a different civilisation.

They had the discipline to control a large organisation, and over and above that, to impose controls on themselves. Having acquired such valuable virtues right from childhood, it was impossible for the middle class to understand why the kids, both black and white, would suddenly explode into the most terrifying rages. It was both alien and embarrassing to the middle class, who were not accustomed to such naked shows of emotions. In the kids it seemed almost schizophrenic. The gap between the moment of calm and the rage was infinitesimal. They could switch from one to the other so fast that it was impossible to predict the happening. A wrong word, a push, a glance, an imagined slight and the boy or girl would explode into fists or pull a knife or a chain. The younger, smaller kids could be held away at arm's length until the rage subsided. The older ones had to be talked to, very fast. One once pulled a knife on Wendy and all she could do was talk until he put it away.

In the Yorkie or the Robert Jones the kids knew if they pushed any of the youth workers they'd get themselves battered. Rage would match rage. None of the ex-Borstal boys in the Yorkie or the black youth-workers in the Jones would react any differently from themselves. Bobby could scream with the best of them.

This was a major problem confronting the Education Department. The middle class knew how to run the clubs but the kids didn't identify with them. The working class could identify with the kids but couldn't manage the clubs.

White, middle-class girl who has worked in the Blackie from the start: *'I prefer the black kids. When the Blackie was being used by the Skins, it was awful. The white kids were just crude. They weren't able to appreciate anything you did for them and they'd be so destructive. The black kids are gentler. They have a culture—their music, their dances, the way they dress—which the white kids just don't have. In a way, I feel far sorrier for the white kids. They really do have nothing.'*

The Blackie was crowded that night, and the soul sounds reverberated through the old church. Radio Doom, the Blackie disco, was on full power. It was as professional as any radio station. It had not only turntables, but tape-decks as well–all the best equipment. All the Yorkie and the Jones had was a rectangular box with two turntables, an amp and speakers. Some of the kids were dancing. The others fooled around playing basket-ball, wrestling, rapping. In the basement, Wendy was running sewing classes and Bill was directing the video-taping.

Neither Marko, Ato nor Alan danced. Marko, after mooching around for fifteen minutes, went out to sit on the steps. He could smoke a joint in peace; they didn't allow hash in the Blackie. Ato and Alan ricocheted from corner to corner. Playing games when the urge took them, rapping, arm-wrestling. There were about a hundred kids in the Blackie and some of them were waiting for 10.30, when it closed. Then they would fight the Park Street Boot Boys.

Bicklo was particularly strutty that evening. He'd had a few bevvies in the Furnace pub after work. He'd spent a good chunk of his pay and returned home rolling slightly. He'd sobered up after tea. The good feeling was still in him, though, when he jogged across to the Yorkie.

It was packed. The majority of the kids were in the disco dancing to a song of Gary Glitter. The others shuttled continuously between floors, the disco and the street. They would play table football for fifteen minutes, snooker for half an hour, spend five minutes in the disco, swing from the rope in the gym, and sit out in the street rapping. There was as much activity on the street as in the Yorkie.

John Warren was on the door when Beno and Peter drove up in an Avenger, parked it five yards from the door and began to walk in.

'For fuck's sake,' John said, 'don't park that car outside the door.'

Beno looked hurt. 'Only going to be ten minutes, John la. The pigs don't know I've screwed it yet. Just took it off Duke Street.'

John shrugged. It was difficult to make them understand. You couldn't lecture them. If you did they'd never come back.

All John could tell them was to suss everything out before they did the screw. He spoke from experience. He was one of them. He'd been born in the same tenements, hung around the same streets. He'd first been picked up by the cops by mistake, after a pub fight. Like most of the kids, he decided that if they were going to grip him for something he hadn't done he might as well get gripped for a job he had done. He stole a car and the pigs gripped him for taking and driving and possessing a stiletto. They fined him £35. He was on the dole and couldn't afford to pay so they sent him down for a while.

When he came out John was well set to follow the normal pattern of a boy's growth. First the mistaken arrest, next the deliberate crime committed out of a sense of martyrdom, then the bust. And after a prison sentence an attempt to earn a living as a petty criminal. By chance John became an exception. One evening in a pub he met a detached youth-worker who talked him into devoting some of his time to the Yorkie. At first John would drop in only in the evenings and help out. The settlement then made him a part-time youth-worker. Finally he became a qualified, full-time youth-worker.

John's relationship with the kids is different to Jimmy Smith's. Jimmy is also from the neighbourhood but he never got himself into serious trouble. Jimmy bases his relationship with his charges on the ability to challenge and beat the kids at any of their sports—snooker, table tennis, football. John's is based on his experiences; he is one of them, he's done the fighting, the

66

screwing, the time. They know, when he tells them to suss out a place or how to behave in court, that he's talking from personal experience. John is a short-bearded man with a barrel chest. His arms, because of his chest and lack of height, look extra-long. He's strong. Strong enough to wrestle with the older kids and hold them hard enough to make it hurt. He's a good-natured, easy-going man who laughs easily.

'Well, when they come and question me about who that car belongs to,' John said, 'I'll tell them to come and ask you. Right?'

'Go on. You wouldn't do that to me, John la. Anyway, they're too stupid to ask that question.'

'Don't you believe that, you stupid bastard,' John said. 'It's you who's stupid if you think the pigs go around with their eyes closed.'

'Piss off,' Beno said angrily and ducked into the Yorkie.

John shook his head. How many times do you tell them? He knew he could have made Beno move the car. It would only mean a hundred yards up the road, and the break in a relationship. How many times to tell them? The pigs made raids on the Yorkie whenever a car was stolen or a house screwed. They never even bothered about a warrant. Only last week they'd pulled up in their Land-Rover and before you could move two of them had dived into the disco and come out with Pete. They put him in the back of the Rover and questioned him for fifteen minutes while John and Bill bodily held the kids back in the Yorkie. Then, only a few days ago, that stupid bastard Terry and a couple of other twelve-year-olds had stolen a car from outside the cathedral. It had been a wet night and the cobbles outside the Yorkie glistened like greased nipples. Terry came down the road at thirty, slammed on the anchors and skidded into five parked cars. The pigs spent an hour outside the Yorkie. They knew where the culprit was and also knew it was hopeless finding him. John had made Terry wipe the steering-wheel clean of prints.

At nine o'clock a fight broke out in the disco. It was between two pussies, Jean and Dee. The word reached John only seconds after the first slap and he and Billy ran in to separate the fighters. It had to be done quickly. A fight was like a spark. Two would become three, four, a bush-fire of fists and furniture suddenly consuming the whole building. John grabbed one beef, Billy the other, and pushed them out on to the street. That didn't stop the fight. Jean already had her left eye puffed and black. The other kids all spilled out of the Yorkie and in a moment there was a suffocating circle of a hundred boys and girls surrounding the two fighters. They screamed and scratched. John tried to step between them, as he did with the boys, and retreated after one attempt, having had his hair and his beard pulled and a swelling bruise inflicted near his kidneys.

'I swear', he said as he sat on the steps, 'I'll never separate two pussies fighting, ever again.'

Nobody else tried. They only egged the girls on, wanting to see the eye split wider, the hair pulled harder. Finally, after fifteen minutes of screaming, Jean was dragged down Nile Street by her friends.

'What was it about?' John asked Trevor.

'Jean thought Banner was her feller. Then Dee cut in. Jean slapped Dee.'

'Fucking Banner.'

'It weren't his fault la. He says he wasn't interested in either of them.'

'Like fuck.'

Dee was trying not to cry. She sniffed and shook her head. Tear drops cut a shining line down her cheeks. She was a pert, cheeky girl with short, blonde hair which was now straggly. She had a faint scratch on her neck. In between her sniffles, she was proclaimed the victor by her friends.

'Where's Banner?' she finally asked.

'He's not stupid, you know,' Bicklo said with a grin. 'Scarpered.'

'I'll kill that bastard when I see him.'

They call us 'beef'. It's a horrible word, isn't it? Not as nice as 'chick' or some other word. 'Beef' and 'pussy'. To our faces. It makes us feel like cows. We don't have any word for them. I wish we did. I can never think of any apart from 'bastard'. You've got to physically fight to stay with them. You've got to hit them back as hard as they do and try to hurt. If you just take it la, they'll step all over you. I'm telling you. Last year, just for a joke, four of the boys caught me and tied me to the railings in Nile Street. They threw mud and shit all over me. Then they threatened to rape me. It was in the afternoon. I screamed and no one came. They undid my blouse and then they changed their minds. I nearly fainted. It was all a lark really. They wouldn't have really raped me.

PROBATION OFFICER: *'The girl in this society is normally more stable than the boy. Her pattern is to finish school and then get a job which she will stick to as long as possible. She's more responsible both to herself and her family. She wants the money for clothes, make-up and everything else.*

However, if a girl cracks up, her behaviour is far worse than any boy's. She will steal, fight, lie, cheat . . . her normal form of rebellion is to get herself pregnant and into deeper trouble. The reason for the crack-up is usually to be found in the relationship with her parents.'

Dee was in trouble with the pigs and on probation. She'd been caught stealing and causing a public nuisance. If they caught her again, they'd send her away.

Jean wasn't gone for long. A small group of women, with her in front, started up Nile Street. The kids waited and watched. Jean's mother, aunt and older sister looked menacing. Dee didn't move. She could get her mother and brothers when the time came. The screaming lasted another ten minutes. When the kids saw that there was to be no action, they lost interest. They drifted back to the Yorkie to wait for the ten o'clock close and the real fight.

'You fightin' tonight?' John asked as Bicklo passed.

'Depends on them niggers la, don't it?' Bicklo shrugged. 'If they fight, we'll fight.'

'Don't give me that shit,' John said. 'What the hell you want to keep fightin' them for?'

' 'Cause they're niggers la. Why else?'

John didn't like the answer. He was married to a black girl and he hated the battling. Many times he'd tried to control them, sometimes even by locking the door until the black kids had passed. It seldom worked. The Park Street mob would go mad and batter their way out of the building. They'd sniffed the spoor and wanted to hunt. Other times, he and Jimmy would plead, cajole, bribe, promise. Nothing worked.

'You phoned the police?' Wendy asked Sally, one of the youth workers. Sally nodded. It was 9.45. The Blackie always phoned the police before they shut their doors. If the police didn't show up on the streets and there was fighting, they could be blamed.

'Who's doing trail duty?'

'Me and Frank,' Sally said. Each night two of the youth workers would walk as protectors with the black kids. They'd walk as far as Windsor Street, where the ghetto began, and like the cops they'd stop on that border. From there it was home territory for the black kids.

Marko was nearly high. He was sitting on the top step of the Blackie, his back against the pillar, with Alan, Ato and Robbie.

They were passing the joint from hand to hand and talking softly. Marko didn't understand every word they said. He felt muffled and warm but every now and then he'd say, 'True, true.'

At the door, the kids were already beginning to line up. The Radio Doom disc jockey was booming out his good-nights. The kids were looking forward to the coming battle. For many, it was a high. A moment of power, of exuberance as they finally confronted their ancient enemy. It was the only time they ever did.

In school, in daily life, at work, he was elusive. He was hidden behind the smile, the polite rejection; sliding and slipping away before the rage had a chance to explode. When it did, it was too late. The moment had gone and the explosion took place within them. In the evening fight it was all different. They could see the face and hear their names being called: 'Nigger. . . . Black bastard.' It was a relief when the façade dropped briefly, and they could return the calls: 'Honky bastard. . . White trash. . . Skivvy. . .'

At ten o'clock the kids began to pour out of the Yorkie. They jammed themselves in the doorway in their hurry to run on to the street. Bicklo placed his boot on Snowy's bum and pushed him through. Chas was more casual. He waited until a younger boy had fought his way to the front, then picked him up and took his place, pushing the boy behind him.

'You comin' la, la' Snowy asked Chas.

'You jokin' la,' Chas said. 'If the fuckin' pigs catch me with a brick in me hand I'm in for two years. I'm going to see my beef.' Chas had been courting for five weeks and it had helped to quieten him. But he didn't hurry away as he should have. He helped Snowy and Bicklo to chase Trenchy.

Trenchy had remained hidden in the disco until the last possible moment. By that time he hoped most of the gang would have moved down to Great George Street. He could then have whipped around the corner and run home. But this scheme was disrupted by Mrs Bickley. Regular as clockwork, Mrs Bickley would stand at the Yorkie door at ten o'clock and wait for her younger sons. She couldn't control Dave and Harry, for they could run faster and further. But the two younger boys were still vulnerable to her slaps. She could whack them hard enough to bring tears to their eyes. She trapped them as they came out of the door and Snowy caught sight of Trenchy as he was sliding past Mrs Bickley.

They chased Trenchy up and down Nile Street. He ducked,

stopped, twisted, running with zip and the energy of a hunted rabbit, as all the kids did. But there were too many in pursuit.

Snowy and Dave held his arms, Chas and Paul his legs. They carried him down to Great George Street. There was a stream of kids, flowing down with them, shouting and chasing each other. Paula, Mary and Dee were skipping hand in hand and singing:

> We're goin' to get the niggers tonight,
> Niggers tonight, niggers tonight.
> We're goin' to get the niggers tonight. . . .

On the corner of Great George Street and Nile Street was a postbox. They carried a struggling Trenchy to it and tied him to it so that, like a sacrifice, he faced the direction from which the black kids would be coming.

The patrons of the Horse Shoe pub across the street had come to stand outside with their pints; the guests in the Lewis Hostel settled themselves comfortably at the windows; the tenants of the council houses stood on the steps and balconies. Everyone knew what was going to happen.

Bicklo and Snowy herded the kids across to Upper Pitt Street. The shadows were deepest there as the street-lamp was always broken. A small force went out to gather bricks, slates and bottles.

Bicklo stood out in front, in his role of King. He had earned his position by pushing himself further and further up front so that the others would see who was the leader. At the moment, however, he was being challenged by Snowy, who was only fifteen, but looked nineteen, and whose ambition was to be called 'King of the Battlers and King of the Robbers'. He was a stocky boy with shoulder-length brown hair and a flat, square face. He was always dressed in brown striped trousers, a white shirt and a striped pullover. Both his shoes had holes in them and his big toes stuck out.

Bicklo and Snowy both were pretenders to a vacant throne. Whacker was in a prison exile and they had a few months to play I'm-the-king-of-the-castle. Once Whacker returned the game was over. Unless one of them had the guts to challenge him.

Whacker! He's totally paranoiac la. He's mad, insane, a psycho case. I'm tellin' you, when he's around, you don't know what to do with yourself la. He's so mad, he keeps you guessin' la. Course, I'm not scared of him . . .

71

but you never know what he's going to do. Look, if Whacker has sweets and offers them to you and you say no, Whacker'll say, 'So you don't like me sweets.' Thump. If you take his sweets, he'll say. 'You always take me sweets.' Thump.

Whacker! Fuck me, he's a mad bastard. Even the pigs stay clear of him la. He's king of the battlers. I seen him fight the pigs once. He kicked one straight in the balls la. . . . It was funny. . . . The bastard dropped like a lump of shite. The other called in four more pigs and five la . . . five managed to hold him. Shite, they battered him. Five to one. That's Whacker. We was walking down Duke Street one evening when we see some niggers comin' down the road. There's me, Whacker, Paul and Dave la. There was least ten of them. And we started battlin' la. Whacker picks up this pole. Weren't even a pole. Was a fucking tree I swear la. I don't know where he got the strength. Whack . . . whack . . . it's all over la. Them niggers ran as if the Devil were chasin' them.

Whacker! Once I tell you we defied him to walk into the Blackie la. The Blackie where there's least a hundred niggers. Anyone walks in there and they're dead. So Whacker says I'll do it. You know what he done la. He had a hand grenade, his dad's from the war. He walks into the Blackie, all cool, and the niggers once they get over their surprise, just goin' t' kill him, when he whips out this grenade. Can you imagine it la. Whacker coolly standin' in the middle with a fuckin' grenade in his hand . . . and he starts to pull the pin. There wasn't anyone in the building in one second. They jumped out the windows. He's paranoiac, I swear to God la.

Whacker was mythological. He existed far bigger and grander than life, for that is the way the Park Street Boot Boys wished to believe him to be. They forced the myth on him and like a feudal warlord he accepted the sword they thrust into his hand. Knowing that whoever held the sword would eventually have to push it into his own bowels.

Bicklo and Snowy were fighting for this vacant position now, though neither was worthy of it. They pushed each other–battling, robbing–but not enough. Little nudges, hoping the other wouldn't escalate too much. The rest of the gang didn't take part in the ritual. They watched, not caring which one won until they saw the victor.

Frankie led the hundred-odd kids out of the Blackie. Like a school crocodile it straggled across Great George Street and up to the last Chinese chippy. The younger kids darted into the chippy to spend their 5p; hurrying on the girl behind the counter because they didn't want to be cut off from the main party.

'Slow down for the young ones,' Sally called from the rear.

Frank did. The others didn't. They flowed on, talking softly, occasionally stooping to pick up a brick or a bottle. Marko found a nice half-brick. It fitted comfortably into his hand. Alan picked up a piece of slate. Ato kept his hands empty.

7

THE leaders of the crocodile were fifty yards now from the triangle on Upper Pitt Street. They could just catch glimpses of shifting shadows, momentarily outlined against a lighted window. It was impossible to tell how many were waiting there.

Years ago the fighting had been territorial. The Park Street boys had fought the Dingle gang with the same ferocity as they fought Toxteth boys. But since the Falkner Place riots, and the new identity consciousness of the black kids, there had been a subtle and dangerous change. If you asked the Skins why they fought, they'd say, 'Territory.' If you asked the black kids, they'd say, 'Racial.' The Skins were in a sense not telling the truth. In the last year there had been no serious fighting between Dingle and Park Street, and quite often a few of the Dingle boys could be seen in the Yorkie, something that had been unheard of eighteen months back. To confuse the watchers in Great George Street more, two or three white boys could be seen fighting on the side of the blacks. These white faces reassured the spectators: they seemed to defuse the danger and misled them into believing that what they were watching daily was just another gang fight over territory. They never studied the faces of the Park Street boys. There were no black faces on their side. The black kids didn't mind the one or two white faces fighting on their side. It amused them. Usually the boys were very close spars of a black kid, and in the neighbourhood you did more or less exactly what your spar did. This gave them a temporary immunity. Exactly how long it would last if the fighting really did get serious was impossible to tell.

Trenchy freed himself as the first boys reached Mary McConnell's sweetshop. He hadn't been tied very well or tightly. He crossed the road to join Dave and the rest of the gang. It was his way of making amends for his earlier reluctance. He knew that a brick or two wasn't that serious, and once he'd made a token effort he'd drift off home. They'd be fighting for another hour or so.

At the corners of Great George, Park and Upper Parliament streets, the darkness was cut by flashing blue revolving lights. There were two police vehicles. One a Herald, the other a Land-Rover. The Herald parked in front of the bank; the Land-Rover raced up Great George Street, made a U-turn and began trailing the black kids. Two policemen on foot stood in between the two groups near the corner of Nile Street.

It was part of the ritual, part of the nightly war-game. The police, once they had been informed, had to be there. They played their role as referees every night for half an hour. But only as referees. They would otherwise play no part in the boys' lives until the time came for making arrests. They were loathed by both sides.

PROBATION OFFICER: *'It's very hard for the police to do their job. When hundreds of boys are milling around you, you just pick up those you think are the troublemakers. Of course, the boys get bitter when they're really innocent and they do afterwards get into real trouble because they're fed up with getting picked up for doing nothing.'*

'Ready, Alan,' Marko whispered out of the corner of his mouth. Alan nodded and tightened his grip on the slate. The leaders of the crocodile had passed the postbox where Trenchy had been tied and were now in front of the Lewis Hostel. The tail was still near Mary McConnell's sweetshop. Marko and Alan were somewhere in the centre. Ten yards in front of them was a shirt-sleeved pig holding his truncheon, which he tapped impatiently into his left palm.

Opposite Marko were the Park Street boys and girls. They were bunched together tightly, and chanted rhythmically: 'Niggers. . . . Black bastards.'

PHIL CANTOR, a solicitor: *'The police often overreact to situations. One example: six black boys were playing football during their lunch hour in Granby Street, the blocked-off end. Some shopkeepers objected and called the police. The boys were doing no harm, and the police told the boys to move along. Four of the boys had never been in trouble before. The boys did move but obviously too slowly for the police, who arrested them on an obstruction charge. It was totally unnecessary. The result of it is that two of the boys have now committed further offences. They would never have done them if*

75

it hadn't been for that first arrest. There are lots of other cases of overreaction.'

'Fucking pigs,' Snowy shouted. 'If you weren't here we'd batter those black bastards.' He laughed and pointed. 'Hey, there's Ato la. Ato,' he shouted, 'what's a whitey like you doing with those niggers.'

Everyone laughed when they saw Ato point to his hair. They all knew he would and the laughter grew louder.

'He's going fucking spare again,' Snowy said. 'Look, there's Marko and Alan la. He's a real evil bastard, that Alan.'

'There's the big nigger I was tellin' you about,' Paddy shouted and pointed.

'That's Carlos,' Bicklo said, once he recognised the ambling walk. . . .

A young woman sociology graduate who works for a national welfare association. She lives in a shabby tenement in Bicklo's territory: *'I really dislike the police. Because I've lived here for three years and know all the kids and the people, they keep harassing me. They pressure me to give them information, which I refuse to do. In retaliation they've been threatening to get me on false charges. They harass the kids unnecessarily too. If, for instance, a shop is broken into and one of the kids happens to be passing, they'll arrest him for it. It is easier to build an impressive arrests record in this part of Liverpool than in any other part of England. I also feel that by arresting leaders, like Whacker, the police make a big mistake. Whacker could control his gang and by removing him you de-control the kids and this makes them more unmanageable. It's very easy blaming the parents for not controlling their children, but tell me what parents today, of whatever class or country, can control his children. My irony is that I, a middle-class girl from Surrey, cannot convince my parents that the police aren't as noble as they think they are. They just don't believe my experiences.'*

On their side, the Black kids also recognised a lot of the faces among the Park Street boys. They pointed to Bicklo and Snowy and Eric Hall. Eric shouldn't have been there. He was a thin, moustached boy with tattoos on the insides of both his forearms. He'd just finished a prison sentence for stabbing a policeman. His ambition had been to go to sea and he'd passed his medical, the final and most important step for joining a ship, when the stabbing occurred. A few days previously, he'd seen his younger brother battered by the police. So when he returned home one evening and saw them searching the flat, his brother's mouth cut and the eye swollen, Eric picked up a knife and in brief, violent rage pushed it into the pig's shoulder. It was his first offence. A police record, however, bars anyone from joining a ship. Eric cried when he knew he could never go to sea.

Eric had been out three weeks now, and he was only watching. It really made little difference whether he threw a brick or not. The pigs had already got him. They'd picked him up ten days ago and booked him for breaking a man's jaw in a pub fight. He swore to the pigs he'd never been in the pub. He knew it would make little difference to the magistrate. If he'd stabbed a pig, he'd also broken the man's jaw.

Ato looked across. He saw Snowy, and because Ato was high Snowy looked, with his arms folded, distorted and misshapen. Like one of those paralytic kids, Ato said later, that you see on the telly. It frightened him at the moment and he stopped to peer into the shadows as Snowy shifted and grew into a more grotesque shape.

MARGARET SIMEY, in an interview: *'The coloured community is fed up with being hounded. No one is safe on the streets after 10 p.m. One gang we know has given the police an ultimatum to lay off within two weeks or they'll fight back. Poor dears. They come and sit here in my flat and ask me, "What are we doing wrong?" I recommend them to read Derek Humphry's book,* Police Power and Black People, *as a start towards understanding what they're doing wrong.'*

Suddenly Marko charged. He held the half-brick tightly in his hand. One step behind him was Alan. Marko reached the centre line of the road before the effect of his move was felt on the crocodile. Like fighter jets rolling into combat, half a dozen black kids peeled out of the formation and barrelled in behind Marko and Alan. Marko hit the other pavement. His right hand was raised and pulled back. . . .

Interview with a policewoman (anonymous) on Radio Merseyside: *'In certain police stations, particularly in the city centre, brutality and drug planting and the harassing of minority groups takes place regularly. On one occasion, I witnessed a police sergeant attack a teenage youth who had reported to the station while on parole. The sergeant poured insults on*

the youth, picked him up by his coat lapels and banged his head against the
wall several times before throwing him into a chair. The youth was then
dragged out to a police jeep and driven away. After hearing the word
"agriculture" used on a number of occasions, I asked what it meant. The
reply was "Planting, but you can leave that to us".' [Derek Humphry,
Police Power and Black People]

Bicklo, Snowy, Paddy, Bill, Jimmy, Beno . . . they all saw Marko
break but they couldn't believe he was going to make the run.
There were eighty of them packed into the square and he was
one . . . two . . . four. . . . They held their ground until Marko
raised his arm. They knew Marko was mad. One of them was about
to be hit by the brick. No one knew who broke first. Suddenly they
scattered and ran, bumping and tripping against each other in
order to avoid the brick. They could glimpse the others coming in
behind Marko. A tight, fast-moving wedge about to drive through
their midst. As he ran, Paddy thought the niggers really had guts.
They had more fucking guts than any of his own side, who were
now scattering down Upper Pitt Street, ducking into doorways,
over walls, up winding stairwells. . . .

BOBBY NYAHOE: '*The pigs are really bad la. You can have a good job,*
and be walking down the street minding your own business, when they'll
pick you up for some screw half a mile away. And when you get into the
court, the beak looks at your black face la, and before you can blink he's
sentenced you. You can be driving a car, and the pigs'll stop you every half
a mile to check your licence. I hear they're going to build a police station in
Toxteth. If that happens, it's just pure dynamite. There'll be a riot.'

Marko hurled the brick into the thick of the Boot Boys. He was
running and it was a wild shot. It flew over their heads and through
a window. He didn't break his stride at the sound of breaking glass
or the scream, 'You fucking black bastards', from an adult. He and
Alan cut through to Upper Pitt Street as the Boot Boys scattered.
Alan threw his slate and it hit the side of the wall and broke. The
other black kids came in behind and threw their missiles but by this
time there was no one in sight. Bicklo was crouched on the first
floor of a nearby block. With him were Snowy, Paddy and Beno.
The black kids, without losing a step, curved back on to Great
George Street. They joined the crocodile and laughed at the
exhilarating rush of adrenalin pumping through their bodies.

'I chased those bastards, didn't I, copper?' Marko said as he walked past the cop with the truncheon.

'I saw you,' the cop said. He studied Marko for a moment as if trying to remember the face. 'Move along now.'

PHIL CANTOR, solicitor: *'The problem lies deeper than just the police. They are only the manifestation. I was in court the other day and the magistrate, a middle-class old English gentleman, wanted to know why the kids were giving so much trouble. I stood up and tried to explain. I know the conditions in Holland because my wife is Dutch. The government there has done so much for its people. There the parents have marvellous crèches financed by the local councils. The Crèches are run by highly trained nurses and teachers. The playgrounds aren't just concrete squares with concrete slides and a concrete sculpture, which is what we have in Liverpool. In Holland they have imaginative parks and the best equipment for the children to play with and learn from. And there are so many other things. So I explained to the magistrate that the Council just isn't spending enough money on the kids. They have absolutely no facilities, no one to look after them while their parents work. Before I could even start, the magistrate turned red and said, "How dare you accuse the Council of neglect. I'd like you to know I'm chairman of the Council." Well, I quickly apologised and said over the years the neglect by the Council. . . . Before I could finish again, a woman magistrate rose and said, "How dare you? I was chairman for the last three years."*

'Tell me, how do you win?'

The buck passes. From parents to teacher to cop to youth worker to councillors to planners to parents. The solution lies not in the fragments but in the whole. Leaving finance aside, no single fragment of the structure can function effectively in isolation, independent of the other elements which make up the jigsaw of the kids' lives. Society is so constructed that talent and capital are channelled into the building of a better car rather than into building a better human being.

The Park Street Boot Boys regrouped. The real fighting hadn't started and they formed their own crocodile and walked parallel to the black one until they reached Park Road.

This time it was the black kids who began it first. It was a chant with only a faint rhythm.

Hooligans! We fought a war for you and look at you.

Hooligans! We've given you free education, council flats, clothes to wear and the dole.

Hooligans! You've got a soft life, you've never had to work as hard as us, you've never been as poor as us, we fought a war for you.

The Park Street Boot Boys on the other side took up the chant.

Hooligans! How do you repay society? You smash up trains, you break windows, you write on walls, you steal.

Hooligans! Why can't you be like us and do the good things we do. Now we have to punish you and send you to jail. You are a nuisance to society.

You're all just Hooligans!

Their words and timing occasionally differed; the meaning remained the same. The collective mind, arcing across the road and over the patrolling cops, harped upon the shared experience of rejection. They had but one mind and on it were chiselled the words of parents, teachers, cops, neighbours, probation officers, youth workers, magistrates, wardens, heard not once but a thousand times. Every moment from childhood to this young manhood was marked by a speech, a lecture, a shout of abuse. The face this collective mind saw over and over again never changed. It remained the same, a mask hanging over them. It was stern, superior and uncompassionate. The mask revealed it had a sense of its own great importance and, in return for what little it had done for them, it expected to exact total obedience. When the mask observed that they had not grown up in its own image, its bafflement turned to rage. In revenge for the nibbles and bites they gave it, the mask scooped them up and ate them whole.

The moment of unanimity reflected in the chanting snapped at the bottom of Great George Street. The black kids turned up Parly; the Boot Boys hurried up St James's Place and cut across waste ground towards Windsor Street. The police Land-Rover stayed with the black kids. It moved in first gear, herding and worrying them on to quicken their pace. Deliberately, they slowed down and strung out even more.

'We're still fucking slaves,' Ato said loudly and spat at the wheel

of the Land-Rover. 'Come here . . . go there . . . move along, boy.
We don't even have the freedom to walk the road any more.'

The driver leant out of the window. 'You. Come here,' he said to
Ato.

'Me?' Ato said in feigned surprise.

'You. Come here.'

Ato shrugged and walked very slowly to the window. He leant
against the side of the Land-Rover and shoved a hand in his
pocket.

'What were you saying?' the cop asked.

Marko, Alan, Robbie, Steve and a dozen others slowly came to a
stop. They drifted into hearing and stood looking up at the sky.

'I was talking to myself la,' Ato said. 'I always do that.' He was a
bit more confident when he sensed the others a few feet away. The
cop glanced at the other boys and lifted his foot off the clutch.

'Don't talk so loud next time,' he said and moved on.

'Yessir,' Ato said and V-signed.

The police escort stopped at the Toxteth sign. The Land-Rover
made a U-turn and waited. The crocodile split into two. A small
group continued straight up Parly. They were mostly the
youngsters and the beef. The larger group turned up Windsor
Street. The police roared away. Their responsibility ended at the
signpost.

The black kids broke. They hurried along Windsor Street,
stooping occasionally to pick up a brick or a slate or an empty
bottle. Ato was out in front, his arms already filled. Marko and
Alan ambled far behind the main group. They'd done their
fighting and Marko was longing for another smoke.

Bicklo had marshalled about thirty of his boys below the railings
of St Martin's. Facing up Windsor Street, he had the school to his
left, and on the right a large block of tenements. They didn't have
to search much for bricks and bottles. The ground was scattered
and broken with the remains of the previous day's fighting.

'We'd better send some down the other side la,' Snowy said. 'To
attack them and draw them away from the main group.'

'I know, I know,' Bicklo muttered. He was having problems
holding his position with Snowy. He turned, but already eight boys
had split down the side of the tenement to cut up to Windsor
Street. They would attack the flank of the black kids, while Bicklo's
crowd faced them.

'There they are,' Snowy shouted joyfully. He took a run as he

81

saw the first silhouette and threw a brick. He was too far away and the brick bounced on the road and shattered. Soon everyone was throwing bricks, slates and bottles. They would take runs at each other, each side retreating and attacking rhythmically. It was so dark that they could seldom see each other unless one or two entered a streak of light falling from a lighted window or flitted quickly under one of the remaining street-lights. They had their spectators. Nearly all the tenement windows were filled with people looking down at the miniature war. Marko threw a brick and then sat down on the steps. Alan was more energetic. He cursed and attacked with the main gang.

'They're coming up Windsor,' someone shouted the warning.

Bicklo's divisionary force had been creeping along the side of the tenement, well protected by the dark, deep shadow. They'd made about a hundred yards of ground. Ato led a charge to clear the flank. The Boot Boys held their ground until Ato and his force were within range and then threw all their missiles hurriedly. They didn't wait to see if they hit. They turned and swiftly disappeared back into the maze of tenements. Ato and his group stopped. That tenement was territory they didn't know.

'Fucking white bastards,' Ato screamed. 'Stand and fight.' A brick skittered across the street and he side-stepped casually.

'The pigs!'

Both sides stepped back into the shadows and dropped their bricks and bottles. The small blue police-car shot down the road. As soon as it had turned the corner, the boys returned to the fighting.

Then, Snowy made a mistake. He ran close to the fence and hurled a brick at the black kids. He stopped to watch it miss them by a yard and to scream, 'Niggers.' He stopped a bit too long. A hail of bricks and slates came flying through the air. All missed him except one. A small stone, half-spent by the distance, banged his left wrist. 'Fucking hell . . . fuck . . . fuck . . .' The pain brought tears to his eyes and he bent double holding onto his wrist. He held it gently, spitting a stream of obscenities which somehow anaesthetised the pain briefly.

The others ran to him. Bicklo and Paddy and Bill half-carried and dragged him away from the fence, and once they'd pulled him to cover they all crowded around. They were like children again. They touched his shoulder, peered at his wrist; each wanting in some way to alleviate his pain. Their faces were worried.

'You okay, Snowy?'

'Take him to the hospital. . . .'

'It fucking hurts la,' Snowy said. 'I think it's broken la. Bastards. It just came la. I was standing there and c-r-u-n-c-h. Fuck.'

'Let me look. . . .' Snowy held out his hand and everyone studied it. There was little to see. Some thought they could see a swelling, others a broken bone. They talked about it for five minutes and wondered whether Snowy should visit the hospital for an X-ray. Snowy didn't want to. He thought he'd wait until the morning to see how it was.

A nurse in the Royal Southern Hospital: *'It always surprises me how they behave. They come in . . . usually Friday or Saturday nights . . . with one or two of the boys in a terrible mess. Bleeding badly . . . broken bones . . . teeth shattered. Everything. There'll be about fifteen or twenty with him for company . . . and they're so . . . tender . . . yes, tender . . . towards that boy. They worry about him and ask questions continuously. You get to see their different personalities. You don't normally because they're all grouped as one mass. One boy can be polite . . . another very funny . . . another can be rude and surly. And, you know, if one gets too rude they'll shut him up. They control themselves.'*

Snowy decided to go home. Even though it was his hand that was hurt, to the boys watching him he seemed to limp as he moved slowly down the slope. The others looked back at Windsor Street. The black kids had thinned out. Maybe a dozen or so were still halfheartedly throwing their bricks. Of one accord, the boys began to follow Snowy, leaving Bicklo with half a dozen who wanted to continue the fighting. To Bicklo it was still early. They'd only been fighting half an hour and returning to a crowded home at eleven didn't appeal to him. He, Terry, Paddy and Bill remained. There was enough of the opposition, and Bicklo wanted revenge for what they'd done to Snowy.

Marko, Ato and Alan were among those who left the fighting. The three of them moved across the waste ground towards Upper Stanhope Street. They stopped at the Monty Carlo to buy 5p worth of chips each. The street was full of people. The pubs had closed and the black community was just beginning to start the evening. They'd be going to the Pun, the Somali, the Nigerian. There were so many places that were just beginning to start up. The black and white hookers were stoking up on fish and chips. At a distance their pimps, smartly dressed, perfumed, very hip in leather coats, were leaning against cars and rapping. Marko kept his ears open and

83

heard everything. The boys drifted from group to group unnoticed as they ate chips and threw 'all rights' out to everyone they knew. Until three in the morning, Upper Stanhope Street would be as busy as Lime Street at noon. Everyone was hustling. Alan had managed to collect 10p. Marko bought some more drag to last him through the long night ahead. White men cruised by very very slowly in their cars, staring straight ahead, yet their eyes were swivelling and popping in their sockets as they watched the hookers. Some were beautiful. Black women with jutting breasts, arrogant, overflowing with an aggressive sexuality which affected most of the men who stood around. Their mouths, eyes, bodies promised a good night of balling if you had twenty sheets. They were the expensive hookers and they knew it. They had the style, class and youth . . . their bodies were young, still unworn by the use of a thousand men and one night stands . . . and they knew they were wanted. It was good being a young hooker on a clear, cool night like this. No calling out for trade. It would come, flowing into their crotches through the night; oiling their egos for another few years until their bodies had begun to sag, and their eyes hardened under the encrustation of make-up, while the wounds inflicted on their bodies by their stud pimps began to be felt deep in their psyche, and the booze began to work its way into their flesh, bloating them out into balloons of skin. The moment would slip by them too swiftly; each thrust of the stranger's cock jerked their age and time of life a dozen notches past their physical age.

At thirty they would be too old already and then they would end up on Granby Street, where the five-sheet hookers worked their tricks. The white men would cruise down the streets and pull up at the kerb. Within a minute, a hooker would be down by the side of his car, her breasts strapped and squeezed and pushed up, the flesh of each bosom powdered and scented to look as if they belonged to someone from the past, her dress so tight you could see the line of her knickers cutting down to her crotch. For five sheets another man could enter her, and notch more time on her.

When they'd finished their chips, Marko and Ato drifted up Carter Street. Alan was hustling a hooker for another 10p for the card-game. It was being played on the first-floor landing of the council house near Carter Street. The landing was grimy, scarred with graffiti, and smelt of urine. There were a dozen boys playing First Call. In the middle of their circle on the floor was nearly 50p. Marko and Ato waited until the hand finished and threw their money in for their cards. They were dealt seven cards each; the remainder of the pack was placed in the centre. They had to make up either two lots of three consecutive cards or two lots of the same number or colour. The seventh card had to be under seven before they could make the first call.

Every black kid knew the game. It was played by the big boys in Carter Street where the pot would run to ten sheets and by the kids with a maximum pot of one sheet. They played it whenever and wherever they could. There was always a game on somewhere. Ato always carried a pack of cards in his pocket and if he felt bored he'd take them out and deal himself two hands of First Call.

'Raas . . . man . . . raas . . .' Ato shouted and flicked his fingers together. He jumped up from the crouch. 'What a hand I got. I'm goin' to win this la . . . cream you bastards. . . . How much in the pot?'

'Fifty,' Marko said. He played the game silently and with intense concentration. He chewed on a match as he studied his hand. Ato capered, while the others, like Marko, stared morosely at the boards. Brian rolled a joint and passed it around. He was banker as he was the only one in the game who worked. He had a job in a carpet salesroom as a porter and earned nearly twenty sheets a week.

The game would last for hours yet, and it wasn't the only sign of life in the area, even though it was close on midnight. The square outside was full of black kids chasing each other, running messages, visiting, rapping, and a constant flow of kids broke the tight circle of the players. Kaye was planning to pull a white, blonde beef of fourteen. She and her spar lived one floor above the card-game. She was pretty and wore white toreador pants and a midi blouse that revealed a gap of smooth, white skin. Each time she and her spar passed, one of the boys would kick them in the seats of their tight trousers for disturbing the game. The girls would spit obscenities but did nothing. It was part of their life to be booted. If they could they would fight back. Whilst the girls were fighting the card-players and dodging their kicks, rapping with Kaye and discussing where to get laid, their mothers were screaming at them from the doorways.

It was Friday night and no one was in a hurry to get to sleep. Life was still to be drawn, the waiting for action was part of the life. You waited for something to break. Maybe a bigger win of the pot, more drag, a beef to screw, a car ride that could end in Manchester,

Birmingham, even London if one of the big boys decided to make the ride, a shebeen hot with music, booze and beef and more drag, a sudden chance to screw a house someone had found unlocked. There was an endless choice of possibilities, fresh and juicy, and you waited for the right one to show up. The card-game, the rapping were all part of the big wait. Everyone was waiting–on the stairs, on the parapets, in the corridors, outside the chippy. There was a tense expectation that somewhere outside each one's vision there was hot action. Sleep and the loneliness of bed would only cheat one of the chance to be part of the action. The grapevine hummed and thrummed with possibilities. A shebeen was being arranged . . . maybe . . . Leesup was making a run to Manchester for action . . . maybe . . . Frankie had been gripped by the pigs for G.B.H. on Upper Parly . . . no, he'd been screwing a car for shite sake when they gripped him and beat the shite out of him . . . wasn't Frankie, was Martin . . . they gripped him for carrying drag. Robbie, all loose and dangly, ran up the stairs.

'Where you been la?'

'Pun.'

'Any . . .thing?'

'Naw. . . . You got any drag? I got fifty p here.' Brian handed him a small finger-nail-sized lump and Robbie ran down the stairs and out into the night. Marko jumped up and called out after him.

'Where you goin' la?' There was a note of expectation in his voice. The promise of. . . .

'Nowhere. Just smoke some drag and. . . .' Robbie's voice trailed off. Marko returned to the game.

He'd had shit-awful luck and he was fed up. He'd lost 40p, had no more bread to spare and only three smokes of drag left in his jacket pocket. He threw down his hand and ran down the stairs. He had a beef in Kimberley Street who he'd met at the Blackie that night. He'd promised to grind her pussy at midnight. She was fourteen and was hot for Marko. A lot of the girls were. He looked so vulnerable and they all wanted to protect him. And then again he had a tough reputation which also attracted the beef whenever he wanted. Her mother was out at the club and they could have a few hours' fucking without any interruption. He went to her because he had nothing else to do. He passed Alan in Carter Street. Alan had managed to hustle together 40p and was going to cut himself in on the card-game.

'Where you goin' la?' Alan called. 'Something promised . . .?'

'Pussy,' Marko shouted and kept running. 'On Kimberley. Later, man, later.'

'Later,' Alan said. 'I'll be playin' cards.' When he got to the game, Ato had just won 30p and was dancing up and down, flicking his fingers together.

Bicklo sat with Paddy on the railings. Upper Pitt Street and Upper Frederick Street, as far as they could see in all directions, were deserted. Now and then a car raced by on Great George Street. Otherwise they had the night more or less to themselves. It was only 11.30 and there was nothing to do. All the kids had gone home. Snowy had bandaged his hand and wasn't going to come out again that night. He would normally jump out of the window once his parents had gone to sleep. The boys on Park Street didn't have a card-game. They had no hookers to stare at, no drag to blow their minds, no shebeens, no wild rides to Manchester or London. Even the chippy was closed.

The fighting had finished half an hour ago. It had moved, almost by common, silent consent, from Windsor Street to Nile Street. There were only half a dozen left on each side and they threw bricks at each other, charging up and down the cobbled slope in the give-and-take of territory. Bicklo had nearly led his side into a trap. Three of the black kids had arrogantly swaggered down Nile Street from the cathedral end. Bicklo had been standing near the postbox outside Lewis's with his group. The temptation to tear the balls off the black kids had been too much. He'd led a charge up, hurling bricks and obscenities, pushing the black kids off his territory. They'd just reached Rathbone Street when Paddy had glanced to his left. Three black boys were silently running in towards them, bricks and bottles ready.

'Run,' Paddy screamed. Bicklo was the first out. If he'd been caught in the trap, they'd have battered him to death. He sweated at the memory of the close call.

He sighed. Paddy and he'd been talking about the fighting for the last half-hour. It gave them both a chance to boast of their courage and what they'd have done if they'd caught a nigger. Now they were silent, surrounded by empty night and with only sleep ahead of them. They wanted to wait the night out but neither had any hope that there'd be action.

'Later,' Bicklo finally said. He jumped off the railing and trotted up Nile Street. As he walked back, kicking stones, he heard the echo of his feet and the rattle of the bricks. He wished there was something else to do, other than returning home.

He pulled the key out of the letter-slot and let himself in. The flat was silent. From the three bedrooms came the muffled, stuffy sounds of sleep. He didn't go straight to bed. He went into the bedroom where his three brothers were sleeping, the beds crowded against each other in the small room, and took out his briefcase. In the front room he opened it and reverently lifted out the heavy *Dictionary of Electrical Engineering* and a notebook. The dictionary was leather bound and weighed nearly five pounds. The engineer he'd worked with as an apprentice had given it to him free. He found a biro on top of the mantelpiece beside the pools coupons and settled down to study. He didn't do this often. Maybe once a week, sometimes not for months on end. It happened when he felt depressed and empty and wanted to recall the past. He would dream he was still an engineering apprentice and as a person had more worth than a porter in a furniture warehouse. He would study for five or ten minutes and then slowly shut the book. The information never entered his mind. His eyes only caressed the figures, the calculations, the tables. He could, at one time, have possessed them, but now they were beyond his reach. He put away the books and the pen and shut the briefcase. 'You had your chance,' his mother would tell him, 'and you mucked it up yourself. You're the only one to blame.'

Bicklo knew he was the only one to blame, but that didn't help. He had been so much luckier than the others. He would have had a good life-good pay, status, a trade. But he'd fucked it all up, and the chance would never return.

The card-game on the stairs finished at three. Marko had changed his luck. The hour he'd spent with the beef had been worth while. She'd wanted him to stay the night–like all beef she had begun to get possessive after the first fuck–but Marko had said 'Later' and slid out of bed. He'd won back his 40p and made another fifteen. Ato still had 20p. Alan had lost all he'd hustled. They were, of course, high. The drag was nearly all finished, and when they left the game they headed for Stanhope Street. They sat on the steps of 116 and rolled the last joint. It was chilly, but none of them felt it. The pale light of coming dawn and the dew in the air passed ghostlike through their ephemeral bodies. They were up there with the stars and growing taller by the moment, slipping past the still buildings like wraiths as they floated over the rubble, the garbage and the broken glass. They could see each other's thoughts, touch each other without moving; all three became one.

The streets were empty now. If there was a shebeen or a car ride, they hadn't heard of it. The hookers were busy in some dark corner of the territory and the chippies shut. An hour passed without them talking or moving. They saw people some-times–spars, acquaintances drifting home languidly–and they waved once or twice. They began the descent gradually and found themselves emerging in a silent, sleeping world. There was nothing to wait for. Whatever had happened had happened without them finding out. They split, Ato down Prince's Park, Marko and Alan down to Windsor Street. If it had been one in the morning, Marko would have taken a cab back to Duff Gardens. It was the only way he could make it back alive. But by this time the white kids were long in bed and he would have the streets to himself.

8

SNOWY burst into Bicklo's room. It was 11.30 in the morning and Bicklo and Jim were still in bed. They had been allowed to lie in by their mother as neither had any particular reason to get out of bed. Bicklo was dozing fitfully, and daydreaming. He would have remained in the stupor for another two hours, until he had to get ready for the three o'clock kick off, if Snowy hadn't shaken him.

Snowy was excited. He had told half the story before Bicklo was completely awake. When he spoke too fast, Snowy spat a fine stream of saliva and paced quickly up and down.

'What are you saying la,' Bicklo sat up and demanded. He wiped his face and pushed Snowy to a reasonable distance. Jim, who'd hoped he wouldn't be woken, sat up as well. It sounded interesting.

'You know Pete la,' Snowy began from the start. 'This morning he screwed this car in Nelson Street. You know la, near that Chink restaurant that's empty.'

'Great Oriental' Dave said.

'That one. This car . . . it's an Escort la, green, and Pete seen it parked there since last night. So this morning he still sees it there and thinks to himself it's worth a screw la. Absolutely no one around la, and he opens it up. Nothing in the glove or under the seats. Then he screws the boot and he sees this box la. . . .' Snowy paused to wipe his mouth, 'and he opens it la. You know what he finds?' He stopped and looked at Bicklo and Jim.

Both shake their heads.

'Jools,' Bicklo guesses finally.

'A fucking camera la,' Snowy said. 'I seen it la. Pete took it home and called me. Not a little camera la, a fucking big one. Lenses, buttons, I think it's a movie camera la.'

'Must be worth least a hundred sheets,' Bicklo said. After a moment of deep thought he added: 'Maybe more la.'

Bicklo wasn't the only one to hear of the theft. By the time he was told, nearly every kid in the territory, and many others as well, knew about it. Snowy was only one of the runners. Word moved more silently and quickly than Snowy could run or talk. A big job like this was never kept to one's self. It was a chance to boast; to attract the admiration of your spars.

Bicklo felt envious as he dressed. He wished it had been him who'd screwed the car. He'd seen it there the day before and had vaguely planned to screw it, but he'd been too busy. Some bastards have all the luck. For the first time he noticed Snowy's hand. The wrist was covered with a grubby bandage.

'How's the hand la?' he asked.

'Okay la. Fuckin' hurts, but nothing broken, I fuckin' hope. Bastard nigger. I'll get him one day. Whoever threw that slate.' Snowy fidgeted and nervously moved round the overcrowded room. He went to the window and stared out. It looked a dull, grey day but the wind was picking up and with luck the sky would clear by the afternoon. Snowy thought of the sunny afternoon. It would be warm and there'd be a slight breeze and he would be able to smell the sea. It depressed him; he didn't want to be in Liverpool today if the sun was out.

'You don't have a sheet to lend me la?' Snowy asked Bicklo, and also included Jim with a glance. 'I swear I'll give it back next week.'

'No la,' Bicklo said and Jim shook his head. 'I just got 40p to spare for the game today. I don't know whether I'm goin' even.'

Snowy followed Bicklo into the kitchen and helped himself to a cup of tea while Bicklo made himself toast. 'I talked to her today la, and promised to see her,' Snowy kicked the cooker in frustration. 'Shite, I just got to go la. She keeps phonin' me and askin' "When you comin', Snowy? I want to see you".' He groaned and sat down. 'You should see that pussy la. You know I don't say a beef is lovely unless I really think so. This pussy la, she's so beautiful I want to cry whenever I think of her and she keeps askin' me when I'm goin' to visit la. Last time she phoned I said "Tomorrow." I swear I tried to get the money la. I went everywhere. I walked down every fuckin' street lookin' for some fuckin' place to screw. I hustled everyone la, and all I got was 40p. I phoned her up la and told her a big lie. I said me brother had broken his arm and I had to take him to hospital. I wanted to cry la. Truly. She's been waitin' for so long.'

The beef lived in Blackpool. Snowy had met her a year ago when he'd made his first ever trip out of Liverpool. He'd worn a new pair of trousers, a jacket and a bright new shirt. And also something he'd never worn before, a tie. There were four spars with him on the day trip and they each had two sheets to spend on the funfair, the pubs and the beef.

It was fantastic! There were millions of people walking on the promenade and they all looked happy. Snowy and his spars had bought cowboy hats, and Snowy walked on the sands in bare feet to feel the earth under his feet. It had been a warm day, and while most of the people were in shirt sleeves Snowy kept on his jacket and tie. He sweated but the tie made him look . . . different.

It was two o'clock in the afternoon that he met her. She'd been walking towards them on the pier with her spar. Snowy had tried to chat up other beef. Some had responded but none were special. For this day he wanted a special beef; and here she was coming towards him. She was the most beautiful thing he'd ever seen in his whole life. She liked Snowy immediately and talked her spar into joining his friends. The rest of the day became a blur. They ate and drank and laughed and talked. He screwed her on the sands in the evening. Her pussy was beautiful; smooth and warm and wet. After the fuck, they'd had a few bevvies and by closing time Snowy was drunk. They'd been fooling around an unfinished swimming-pool, half-filled with water, when Snowy's spar threw a plank across and defied Snowy to walk it. Snowy felt dizzy but he didn't want to look chicken in front of this beautiful beef. The plank had been long and springy. He nearly overbalanced a couple of times. When he reached halfway he heard them all laughing and looked around. One of his spars sauntered up to the plank and kicked it. Snowy fell into the water with his new trousers and shirt. He would have battered the spar to death but the beef put her arm around him and said they'd get away from all 'these kids'. They'd had another beautiful fuck and then Snowy had caught the last train back to Liverpool. He promised her he'd return.

That had been a year ago and he'd never ever been able to hustle enough money to make that return journey to Blackpool. He talked to her often on the phone and each time she asked when he was coming. Snowy in desperation would say 'Soon.' She was fourteen and he was fifteen and the year felt like eternity.

Everyone knew about Snowy's Blackpool beef, and they respected her invisible presence. If Snowy said she was the sweetest, most beautiful fucking pussy he'd ever seen in his life, they believed him. Snowy seldom talked much about beef. Usually he'd fuck them without a thank-you and then call them fuckface.

'What about the place you screwed yesterday la?' Snowy asked hopefully. Chas had told him all about it.

'No money la,' Bicklo said as he swallowed his toast and tea. 'Can't find anyone to buy the shite.' Still munching on the toast, he grabbed his jacket and moved to the door. Snowy sighed and followed. He was determined to raise the money for a trip to Blackpool today.

They half-walked and half-ran to the Prince Albert Gardens tenement block. It was the oldest tenement in the area and as with all the tenements with similar names, 'Gardens' was a tag with a cruel irony. Peter had hidden the camera under a pile of dirty clothes in his cupboard. He was a short, broad boy with eyebrows that met over his nose. He looked worried and nervous as he led Bicklo to his room. Bicklo opened the box; the camera fitted into a neatly designed compartment. He loved mechanical things and he carefully took it out of its case. It was bigger and heavier than he'd imagined. Inexpertly he twiddled the knobs, twisted the lenses and pressed the buttons. Nothing happened. He put it back in the box and shut it.

'You want to buy it la?' Peter asked as they all went out. 'Twenty sheets.'

'No bread la,' Bicklo said sadly. He could have resold it for at least fifty sheets. 'If you sell it la,' Snowy told Peter as they left him, 'lend me two sheets. I swear I'll pay you back.'

Peter promised he would. He wasn't going to get the chance to keep it.

Bicklo and Snowy discussed the camera as they walked to the Upper Pitt Street hangout. Bicklo revised his estimate. He thought the camera was worth at least five hundred sheets, and if he could find twenty sheets he should be able to make a nice profit. Snowy asked him to find twenty-two, and lend him the two.

They were so absorbed in their discussion that they didn't notice anything strange until they reached Great George Street. Snowy froze and looked back and all around him. Bicklo did the same.

'Pigs la, fucking pigs every-fucking-where,' he spat.

They were all in plain clothes and they were everywhere. They were cruising by in unmarked cars, stopping people and talking to them. They stopped Paddy as he came out of his block. Two big pigs, who pushed him against the wall and began questioning him.

Bicklo and Snowy watched for a minute and then hurried to the hangout.

'What's happening la?' Snowy wondered.

'Murder most probably,' Bicklo guessed. He hadn't seen so many pigs that busy before. They sat on the railings and waited, tensely expecting at any moment to have a pig grip them.

Paddy sauntered up ten minutes later. He looked smug, as if he knew what all the pig activity was about.

'Fucking pigs are looking for the camera,' he announced. He folded his arms and leant nonchalantly against the railing. In repose his face, with its two broad, prominent front teeth and its sparse, straggly moustache, looked somewhat like a worried rabbit's. He was obviously satisfied with the impact made by his news. Bicklo and Snowy couldn't understand why the pigs were looking so hard for the camera. They usually sent one car when a house was screwed and then did nothing. Beno and Steve and Bill and a few others began to drift in. Paddy told each one the news; Steve and Bill already knew. They'd been stopped up the road. It was also obvious that Paddy had some more to tell, but was waiting for the audience to grow larger before he dropped the bombshell.

'I sort of acted as if it was the first time I knew about it la,' he began, 'so I just ask the pig, "What's it worth? So many of you bastards running around as if your balls been chopped." The pig nearly batters me see, but I don't care a fuck for him. So he looks at me and says, "It's a very expensive camera and belongs to a T.V. company." Bastards, I says to myself. That's why they're running around shitting themselves. Fucking T.V. company, and it's bad news for all the pigs. They all want to act as if they're Barlow and Dixon. "It's worth," he says to me slowly'–Paddy stopped and took a deep breath: no one moved–' "four thousand pounds." '

'Fuck!' everyone whispered. There was a very, very long silence as they tried to visualise four thousand pounds.

Snowy was the first to surface. 'Fucking four fucking thousand fucking pounds,' he said in awe. 'Fucking thirty sheets is a fucking fortune to me.'

Paddy, however, hadn't quite finished. 'And', he added proudly, 'the T.V. company've put out a reward of fifty sheets for the camera's return. It's in the Echo.'

'Cheeky bastards,' Bicklo said and ran across to Mary McConnell's to buy a paper. They crowded around him while he searched for the item. Paddy was right; it was fifty sheets.

'The pigs'll be picking up every bastard within a hundred miles,' Bicklo said. 'I'm getting the fuck out until they pick up Peter.'

It was as if a bomb had dropped. The dragnet could have pinned any number of minor crimes on the kids. Each had a heavy conscience. They scattered in every direction. Snowy ran back towards home. His hand was throbbing and he didn't have any money as yet. He had to get it; time was running out. He saw Buster walking jauntily towards him; as always, twirling his flute in its cloth bag.

'You got a sheet to spare la?' Snowy begged.

In answer, Buster pulled out his pockets. Snowy sighed again. He told Buster all his problems, and about the camera.

'If I had the money la,' Buster said, 'I'd give it. But no bread la. And if I was that kid–and don't tell me who it is la–I don't want to know–I'd take that camera and throw it far away. Anywhere. It's hot, fuckin' hot. Tell him, Snowy.'

'Not me la,' Snowy said. 'If I even say "all right" to him now the pigs'll grip me. For fifty sheets someone's going to squeal and I don't want to be found anywhere near him.'

He waved and began running again. He thought about the reward. Fifty sheets was a lot of bread. More than he'd ever seen in his life. Fifty sheets! It would take him to Blackpool in style. He could buy himself new gear, buy her the best dinner and beautiful presents. Her eyes would pop when she saw him flash a roll of fives. He passed a telephone. All it would need was one phone call; and no one would ever know about it. Snowy stopped running.

Buster shook his head. The whole territory knew the pigs were looking for the camera. Someone was going to squeal. He continued on his way to the Settlement. Buster was a small, black man. His ears stuck out like cup handles and his nose was crooked. His forehead was very high and his eyes large. Yet in spite of his physique Buster was an attractive man, for his passions raised him high above the others. He loved his flute, which he carried wherever he went. He would play to himself softly, mesmerically, when he felt happy or when he was depressed. As well as music, he had taught himself sculpture. In his room on the top floor of the Settlement, where he worked as an odd-job carpenter, were two African heads. He'd found the chunks of wood in a yard down by the docks, real African wood full of deep lines, grains and knots, and then had carved the heads. A gallery-owner in Amsterdam who'd seen the heads was begging him to send them over for exhibition. Buster couldn't make up his mind. He discussed this problem, as he talked over everything else in his life, with anyone who'd listen. Buster loved talking. He would talk about society, about prison, L.S.D., politics, art and his own confusion. This last occupied him the most. 'The whole fucking world's pure pressure la,' he'd say often. 'I sometimes feel my head is going to burst open trying to understand everything I see and hear. Pressure, pressure. . . .'

Buster, however, wasn't all that different. He'd done eighteen months in prison for causing grievous bodily harm. The pigs had been battering a spar of his, and Buster had gone in to help. He and the spar got away, but a week later, as he was walking down Duke Street, someone had put the finger on him and the pigs gripped him. He swore it was the last time he'd ever help anyone.

He was born and raised in the black ghetto. Like Marko he'd spent all his money and time smoking drag.

'I ate nothing for years la,' Buster would tell listeners. 'I just smoked drag and walked around and around doing nothing. I never left the fucking ghetto for months at a time la. It was so warm and safe and secure and I didn't have no pressure at all. I just smoked and dreamed la. It's like lying in a womb. A black, stinking narrow womb. You want to live in it forever. It's secure and full of your own people who are doing exactly what you're doing–nothing, just feeling sorry for themselves. They smoke drag, fuck every beef they see and cry to themselves. One day I suddenly woke up la and asked: What am I doing? I'm wasting life. If I stay in this ghetto one more day, one more hour, I'm finished. The moment I thought that I packed my flute and walked out. I'll never go back; it's living death.'

Buster would visit the ghetto often. His friends were still there, but he never moved back. He lived in Nelson Street in a council house with his white wife and his grandfather. The pressure here was different. It was Boot Boy territory and, though they granted him immunity, he knew it was only temporary.

'You never know when they're suddenly going to turn on you la,' Buster would say. 'There are a hundred of them and only four or five of us. We'll have no chance.'

Apart from Buster, the 'us' included three other black men working for the Settlement. They helped in the running of the Yorkie and the kids would try their best to remember not to use the word 'nigger' when they were within hearing distance.

96

It was Saturday and Buster planned to spend a few hours working on a new carving. He'd found another chunk of African wood and was carving a man and woman intertwined.

Outside the Yorkie door were half a dozen kids. They were sitting on the steps, leaning against the wall, fooling around. Though the Yorkie never opened on Saturday or Sunday, they'd always be there, hoping that this day would be an exception, that the doors would magically open and they'd be sucked off the streets. When finally they realised that the door wasn't going to open, they'd break in.

The Settlement spent thousands of pounds on security both for its own building and for the Yorkie: new locks, new bolts, new doors, new screens for the windows, new steel and iron wherever it could be fixed on in the shape of bar or sheet. It made little difference. The kids still broke in. Through windows, roof or doors; they even kicked in part of the wall once. There was little of value to steal from the Yorkie–in the Settlement there were typewriters, tapes, radios–but the entering of the Yorkie was a primeval urge. It was a place of shelter, of security. They knew the Settlement would never report them. If it had, the kids would totally lose trust.

'Well, come on, tell me what happened then?' Frank impatiently asked Trenchy. They'd been interrupted by Buster and a discussion about the camera.

They were both leaning against the door of the Yorkie. Frank was a thickset boy with short, curly, brown hair. He had a narrow face and stood and walked with a heavy stoop. He put out his hand and touched Trenchy's sleeve and held on: Frank was blind. His eyes were squinting, milky slits and he depended for direction and guidance on one of the kids. Today it was Trenchy's turn. They would all help Frank in some way or other. Lead him home when he became tired, talk to him patiently, crack jokes with him and good-naturedly rough him up as if he had the gift of eyesight as they had.

'I didn't battle the whole time like Bicklo and the others,' Trenchy said. He told Frank as much as he could. He hadn't thrown any bricks or screamed obscenities. He'd spent five minutes with the gang after escaping from the postbox, and then slowly drifted home.

Frank loved battling, and he wished he could take part in it all. The battling and the screwing. A couple of times he had. He did get into one battle in Windsor Street but as it moved away he'd been left behind. The niggers caught up with him as he stumbled around, but after seeing he was blind they moved on with their attack. It was a humiliating moment for Frank. He had heard, sensed and smelled them around him. Niggers have a peculiar smell and their movements are lighter than white kids'. Frank had waited with a brick in one fist, turning round and round on himself like a trapped animal trying to face its hunters. He had felt a flick on his jacket and threw the brick with all his might. He heard it hit the road and bounce, each bounce growing weaker until it stopped. He wasn't afraid. He would kick and bite and scratch when they closed in. They didn't.

'C'mon,' one of the niggers had said and they'd run softly away in pursuit of his spars.

Another time they'd taken him on a screw. He'd been part of the break-in and tried his best not to be a burden. The boy who led him by the arm had whispered a running commentary of what was happening. As they were getting away, the pigs had suddenly pounced and Frank lost his guiding arm. He heard his spars running and stood there waiting. One of the pigs gripped him roughly, but when he saw Frank was blind, told him to go home and not get mixed up with those 'bastards'.

Frank felt frustrated. They were the only friends he had and he couldn't be a part of their life. So he would listen to their stories. Greedily absorbing their adventures, their victories, their defeats, their pain, their excitement through his ears. His blindness, however, gave him one advantage. In spite of himself he wasn't a part of their life and this saved him for a career. He was a musician and he was going to be a piano-tuner.

'Who all were battlin' for us?' he asked Trenchy.

'Bicklo, Bill, Jimmy. . . .' Trenchy reeled off the names.

'And who were battlin' for them? You see Marko or Ato or that bastard Alan? He's a bad nigger. Was Steve there or. . . .' He knew them all by name and reputation.

'They were all there,' Trenchy said.

'Then what happened. . . .'

Trenchy didn't know and Frank turned to the others. Bill told him about this huge rock hitting Snowy's hand. Snowy's wound was an achievement. It gave him lustre.

'Who threw the brick?' Frank asked. 'You see the nigger?'

Bill shook his head but repeated the rumour he'd heard as if it

were a fact. 'I never saw la, but Paddy said it was Marko. He saw
him throwing a brick just a second before Snowy got hit. We'll
batter that nigger to death for what he done.'

Whether Marko had hit Snowy with his brick or not made little
difference. It had become fact and now another vow of vengeance
would be sworn against Marko. The wisps of guesses such as this
had hardened over the years to become unshakeable facts. Myth
became history, not legend. Marko could kneel at the feet of God
and swear he'd never thrown that brick, battered that boy or
screwed that house, but no one would believe him now. He was
frozen, like Whacker, in the cold ice of reputation.

Marko woke very late on Saturday. It was two when he finally got
out of bed, dressed and dropped Osibisa on the turntable. His aunt
sat in front of the telly, watching the racing. She would bet the odd
bob on the horses. Marko's music drowned out the commentator,
but though his aunt sighed she never objected to what Marko did.
She was putty in his hands; and vice versa.

'Do some shopping for me, Ivor,' she said. 'The list is on the
table.' Marko scanned the scribble as he made himself a cup of
coffee. When he was ready, he picked up the shopping-bag and
shoved a poker into it.

His headache started again when he stepped out. He tightened
his grip on the poker. He'd had to use it more than once while
shopping near Duff Gardens. The Boot Boys would make a
sudden swooping hit and sometimes hardly gave him the chance to
draw the poker. He took his battering when they caught him.
Curled tight as a ball with his woolly head protected by his arms
and his balls drawn deep in between his thighs. Over the last three
months, however, there'd been no attacks. It didn't ease his
headache; it only increased in intensity because it meant they were
waiting and watching. He quickly went round the shops–milk,
bread, baked beans. Two Boot Boys watched him on his way down
Grafton Street. Marko wanted to run. Deliberately he slowed down
to a saunter back to the flat.

He froze when he saw the handbag. It was on the floor just inside
the hallway. He took a deep breath and prepared his face. His eyes
became blank and distant; his mouth straight and firm; he was
visibly withdrawing deeper and deeper into himself. His body
remained a protective shell. He walked into the front room.

He saw his aunt first. She was standing near the window and

99

made a face to warn him of his impending danger. He nodded calmly.

' 'Lo Mum,' he said softly and tried to edge his way to the kitchen.

His mother was standing with a broom in her hand. She was white and in her mid-thirties. She could have been a pretty woman. However, she was too thickset and her face, without make-up, looked sullen. It was a square face, unlike Ivor's, and her auburn hair was cut short. She was dressed, for a woman of her age, dowdily.

'You're back, are you?' she said softly. 'I've got to do all the work around here, haven't I, you black bastard. A nigger like you wouldn't think of helping an old white woman.'

'Sure, mum,' Marko whispered. He didn't move; he even seemed to have stopped breathing. It was as if he were face to face with a savage animal that would attack at the slightest movement.

His mother lifted her broom and took a step towards him. Marko didn't flinch. It was her normal line of attack. She didn't know he did all the cleaning in the flat; his aunt was too old for the work.

'Nigger,' his mother spat. 'You really hate me, don't you, because I'm a lovely white woman and you're black as Hell itself. You hate your mother because she's got beautiful white skin.' She caressed her arms and crooned softly. 'Smooth and white. White.' She jabbed him in the chest and wiped her finger. 'Huh. This nigger thinks he's a man. Showing off all that ugly black skin. You haven't got balls, you black bastard. I've grabbed them and twisted them off.'

Marko nodded. The words were bouncing off his barricaded face. She couldn't hurt him any more, for he was far beyond pain. If it could have been seen, his soul would have been discovered to be a fistful of dried blood and crushed and broken flesh. She had shredded and killed him a very long time ago. Psychically, his frame could take a billion-volt shock from her, from any white person. The first words he'd heard as a child were her obscenities, the first passion he'd been immersed in with his christening-waters was hatred.

Marko had hated his mother. But the first emotion he had felt, long before the hatred, before he could even think or articulate, was fear. When he was two she had placed him in front of the gas-fire and turned on the gas. He'd been saved by his aunt. That moment when his mother had laid him down, his hands as they reached out must have touched barriers of hatred so intense that his fists withdrew in the instinctive cowering fear of children and animals. All his life he was condemned, subconsciously, to this fear, not only of her but also of all white people.

He no longer hated his mother. Hatred fed on passion and energy and at the age of sixteen he no longer had either. He was too old, too wise and too cynical, which was why it was too late for Parky to teach him to like the white man. His mother had taught him otherwise first.

'Don't you shout at Ivor in my house,' his aunt said. She moved forward and placed her old body between them.

'He's my son and I'll do what I like,' his mother shouted. The confrontation between this old woman he adored and a mother he'd hated was as old as his fear. 'I'll kill that nigger. Now get out of the way.'

His aunt refused to move. She couldn't understand her sister's madness. Madness, yes, that was what it was to her. Their mother had been an ancient Irish woman full of booze and goodness, and that joyful womb had spawned a mad child. 'Mad, my sister's mad,' she'd tell Marko. 'God will punish her.'

Marko doubted whether God would take an interest in their life; He never had before. Marko's vision of God was bleak. As a young boy, he had attended the Catholic church regularly with his aunt and prayed often. God had never heard him. There was neither punishment nor reward meted out to him or to his aunt. In the end it was God's indifference to his aunt that broke the tenuous relationship. Late one night Marko had been woken by knocking on the wall from his aunt's room. When he entered she was swaying and fell straight into his arms. He rushed her to hospital with a heart attack. God shouldn't have allowed that to happen to his aunt; God wasn't very cool.

Marko's aunt could understand the pain of her sister's abandonment by her African lover, but not the vindictive hatred that had subsisted in her these sixteen years. She had hounded Ivor ever since the court had handed him over to his aunt. Before that, Ivor had already spent three years in a foster home with his half-brother and sister, his mother's children by another black lover. When Marko was old enough and had begun to earn a little money from his newspaper rounds and his screws, he would spend it all on taking his half-brother and sister out of their 'prison'. The money went on small presents, day visits to the zoo, taxi rides. His half-sister looked very much like him and he had a special affection for her. She had the same delicate face and the same fragile beauty and sadness. One day his mother found out what Marko and his aunt were doing and screamed so many obscenities at the foster home that they would not allow Marko to take his half-brother and sister out any more. He visited them still, and quite often his mother would also be there on the same day. Not out of love, Marko felt, but out of spite, to spoil his day. When the children saw them both, they would run to embrace him and his aunt, and avoid their mother. It only made things worse.

'All right nigger, you go hide behind a woman's skirt,' his mother said at last and stepped aside.

Marko didn't listen to her monologue while he put away the groceries. He knew that if he kept quiet she would finally tire and go away. She did, and he didn't look up until the door slammed. He moved straight to the player and dropped a Jimi Hendrix on the turntable. His aunt touched him. They stood silently together and looked down the side of the tenement to Grafton Street. A few minutes later his mother came into sight. Maybe she felt their eyes piercing her back for, after walking a few yards, she suddenly turned and looked up before either could draw back. They could see her mouth moving and then her hand shot up and made a V-sign.

'Mad,' his aunt said. 'I tell you she's mad. Come, Ivor, I'll make you a nice cup of coffee.'

9

ATO, dressed in paint-stained jeans and a sweater, sat on the arm of the sofa drinking tea. His mother, wearing a dressing-gown that had fallen open to reveal the soft insides of her thighs, was recovering from the night before. She looked older and tireder; the harsh morning light cut new fissures and wrinkles into her face.

'Are you going today?' Ato asked.

'Where?' Annie feigned innocence and stared at the television set. It was a children's programme and she watched it in total concentration.

Ato groaned dramatically and held his head. 'The Housing Office,' he shouted. He was angry and growing more frightened of the lice. He'd had a nightmare that the lice had entered his brain and were eating their way out. He'd read a sci-fi short story once in which these small creatures had entered the bodies of two earth astronauts and taken control of them. It frightened Ato to think that maybe the lice were really alien invaders who were waiting to take control of him. He told Annie about his nightmare.

'You've been watching too much telly,' Annie said in disgust, 'and reading those silly books of yours. You shouldn't believe in all that, John.'

'Well, what do you want me to believe in?' Ato asked. 'This fucking place's driving me mad. So I live in a fantasy. The only trouble I have is distinguishing between my own fantasy, and the telly's and the books', and then this fucking fantastic place.'

Ato found television cruel. It stood in the corner of the room and was continuously on. The sound was barely audible and he would look at it in snatches–as he was passing by, having a ciggie, rapping. It ran from morning till night and he knew he wasn't any exception. It was the same with all his spars. He never watched anything in particular. The shifting, sliding images were as much a part of his furniture as the flying ducks were in his mother's old home. Those mass-produced, fake china ducks, trapped in eternal flight to some paradise that lay beyond the four walls of the narrow, back-to-back houses with their outside privies, were the visual symbols of movement, which the middle class mocked, the poor never had. Today the hip-high shifting picture is the symbol of perpetual motion, of escape down an Alice in Wonderland hole that is right in their front rooms. Escape is never possible; the symbol remains, like those ducks, static in a corner of the room. Ato never watched the documentaries or the 'real' plays or serious films. He loved the dancing, the singing, the adventure stories and yet he hated every new image that rose in front of him. It was envy more than hate. He wanted everything he saw. It promised him so much. The beauty of women, the beauty of objects, the beauty of a landscape, the beauty of a home; the wealth of success, of fast cars, of yachts, of jet rides to magical islands where the sea and the sand and the sun were always perfect. It showed him a rich, shining, happy world which was in direct conflict with the drabness of his existence. Television was to Ato like having a knife picking and gouging at the reality of his life, shredding his brain into a bleeding, suppurating mass. It revealed his inadequacies, his failures, his rotten pinchpenny poverty from which he could expect little respite or escape.

As he became angrier with his mother, Ato became more nervous and jittery. He couldn't sit still as he swore and cajoled her.

'You've got to go today,' he shouted.

'I'm not feeling like it,' Annie said.

'Just thinking of those lice makes me want to die,' Ato pleaded.

'I promise I'll go on Monday, and sit there the whole day. Now I've got a headache, so for God's sake shut up.'

Ato kicked the sofa hard and hurt his toe, but refused to show the pain and ran out of the flat. His blood was boiling and he could feel it burning his skull and steaming through his veins. He struck the wall. His knuckles flinched and bled. He wanted to attack . . . something . . . anything. The energy he spent fighting, destroying, kicking was a release valve for his frustrations. After a fight he would feel as he did after a fuck or smoking hash. He just couldn't keep juggling with the conflict of reality and fantasy within his mind for too long. It was destroying him.

He half-ran and half-walked to Upper Stanhope Street. There was menace in his frustration. It was at these times that he approached danger to see if it would harm him. His spars were the same: they would all try tempting danger.

Ato began to walk on the road. He waited until a fast moving car approached and then stepped as near to it as possible. He allowed the metal to brush his sleeves, scrape against his trouser legs, touched it so that the tips of his fingers stung with friction. He wanted to see how brave he was, to allow the pain that had built up in him to escape into the vehicle. He repeated the move for every car and bus that passed him on Prince's Avenue. He was trying to earth his pain by playing with death.

The rage had extinguished itself by the time he reached Upper Stanhope Street. He felt calm and at peace. Upper Stanhope Street was crowded. The inhabitants of the ghetto had shaken off their long sleep, washed the fuzz of booze, of drag, of sexual combat, from their faces and bodies. It was a new day to be spent eagerly. For the middle-class world outside, the sun was halfway in the sky and a morning had been spent productively at work, at shopping, at playing. It wasn't to be frittered away in bed, in lounging on a street rapping about the night before and the night to come. In the pubs, the pints tasted sweet as they washed away the decay of sleep. The betting shops were busy as bazaars. Black and white men shuffled in and out, their fingers clutching tightly to their small, pathetic bets–25p, 50p. Sometimes, if the horse was hot, seen in a dream or hallucination, it would be a pound. The big boys were in a circle round the steps of Carter Street playing First Call. Ato watched the game for fifteen minutes. His fingers caressed the coins in his pocket; he wished he had enough to join the game. He drifted up to Parly.

He passed the post office, a tiny, well-barricaded, multi-locked, steel-barred room with an iron-and-glass counter. The protection was necessary as it had been broken into frequently. Opposite it was a grocery store; the vegetables looked fresh and delicious, and Ato was tempted to screw one but changed his mind. He went into Ali's and bought a bar of chocolate. He sat on the steps of an abandoned house and slowly munched it.

WHITE SHOP-OWNER: *'I think this whole place stinks. I've been here ten years and just can't take it any longer. They're all animals. How can I like them? I've tried. Oh God, I've tried. Some of the coloured people are perfect gentlemen and women but the others. . . . Especially those half-caste kids. They threatened the life of my son, you know. They came here to rob*

*the place and they took my son as a hostage and threatened to beat him up
with a hammer. They've even beaten me and I've had a nervous breakdown
once already. How can I like them when they did that to me? The whole
place stinks. You try to be nice to them and they attack you. I leave my car
outside and they kick it or hit a football against it deliberately. When I go
out and ask them politely not to, they just do it more. They are the lowest
people in society. It's the white prostitutes and lower-class working girls,
who've married these coloured men, they just don't know how to bring up
their families. Of course, I've reported the break-ins to the police . . . often.
What can they do? Do you know what they call the police in this place. The
name for a policeman is pig. Pig!*

Ato lingered for half an hour on the steps watching the street.
There were many others, sitting on other steps, leaning against
lamp-posts, doing the same thing. It was a popular pastime. You
saw a lot if you kept your eyes open. Gary, Ato saw, was trying to
sell a car stereo. He watched him move from person to person,
pulling the stereo from under his coat as if he were a magician with
a rabbit.

'How much la?' Ato asked when Gary neared him.

'Five sheets,' Gary said. 'It's brand new.' He came and showed it
to Ato, who examined it very carefully before handing it back.

'Four sheets, then?' Gary said.

'Got no bread la,' Ato said and stood up. Gary didn't linger. He
moved quickly to the next person.

Ato decided to visit the Robert Jones. There would be other kids
there. He repassed the post office and Ali's and the chandler's on
the corner of Upper Stanhope and Berkeley Streets. He was aware
that he was being watched by the shopkeepers. Ato was the
vanguard for the hordes that terrified the shopkeepers more than
the Mongols the ancient world. Ato was the one who'd make
sudden raids on their citadels, steal, attack, destroy with no reason.
Ato was robbed of his identity by their hatred. For the shopkeeper
he had no face, no name; he was only a half-caste kid. One was as
bad as the other.

There was music coming from the Jones. Not recorded either,
real live sounds. Ato ran excitedly up the steps. There was no one
in the front room. The sounds were coming from deeper in the
house. Drums, African drums. He could feel and sense the beats,
more than hear them. He moved hurriedly through the maze of
rooms. The drums were loud now, their vibrations were coursing

through his body. He wanted to dance, to obliterate himself in the music.

There were fifty young kids crowded in a back room. Ato couldn't get past the door for the crowd. He pushed and shoved until he could catch a glimpse of the gig. Two black men were playing tall, narrow drums, while five others, three of them women, were dancing. Ato knew they were African. He knew instinctively. They looked proud, and their music and the way they danced were different from anything he'd ever seen. He asked Ramon who they were and she whispered that they were an African folk group. He watched mesmerised for half an hour. They danced the Lion Hunt, Sharpeville, Puberty, Harvest and Courtship. Like the others, Ato felt envious. He had nothing to dance about; no ancient tribal tradition that gave the men and women in front of him such dignity. He was empty. When the dances finished, the Africans asked some of the kids to join in. Ato hurried to the front. He wanted to dance like them, shuffling slowly and majestically over the lino floor. None of them could imitate the Africans. Their blood stirred, their muscles and sinews strained to be African, and it was impossible. They were too far away; they'd been lost over the centuries. Ato touched one of the Africans gently. It was a sad, hopeless gesture. The touch was involuntary and brief. It was his forefather reaching out from his cosmic grave to tell the African: 'I am you . . . I am you.' It's too long ago, and the voice is too weak. No one heard as Ato drifted back to join the kids and watch the Africans dance the Lion Hunt again. Their faces were rapt. They could feel the African sun on their backs, the earth against bare feet, smell the evening African breeze, hear the beasts moving through the tall grass. Ato left before they finished. The pavement seemed extra hard under his feet, and there seemed to be more dust in the air he breathed. These were his only memories.

Bicklo leant against the balcony and looked down on the yard. He'd been in the same position for nearly an hour. He'd watched the children playing in the yard, and the endless stream of traffic on St James's Road. Occasionally he'd heard the pigs were still looking. He wished to fuck they'd find the camera and get out. No one was safe on the streets until they'd gone. He saw Trenchy coming in to the yard.

'Trenchy!' Bicklo called down. 'You seen Snowy la?'

Trenchy shook his head. 'No. But Paddy said he saw him up on Duke Street.'

'What the fuck he doin' there?'

Trenchy shrugged and waited for Gerald to run across and join him.

'Where you goin'?' Bicklo asked.

'Kung Fu la,' Trenchy shouted and mimed the kicks and chops. 'Called "Chinese Connection" or something.'

They all loved the Kung Fu films. The constant, violent action was intoxicating. They never took it seriously though. It was a marvellous dance of destruction and they would cheer and laugh as the hero whirled and twirled, as he knocked out thousands of his enemies. They identified more with the action than the hero. Behind Lime Street Station the new Bond film was running. None of them wanted to see that. Bond was a middle-class hero. His weapons, his women, his clothes, his accent fulfil only the fantasies of the middle class. Bicklo couldn't identify with Bond–a public-school man, a commander in the Navy, a protector of middle-class people–nor with Bond's actions, for he used mainly gadgets to defend himself, while Bicklo only had his hands and feet.

'I'm going tomorrow la,' he shouted as Trenchy and Gerald drifted out. 'Tell me what it's like.' They waved and turned the corner.

There was one film Bicklo had really loved; *A Clockwork Orange.* It was a cool picture and Bicklo had seen it, with his whole gang, twice. They decided after the second time that they would become Clockwork and twenty of them dressed in those white uniforms and bowler hats, with boots and swagger sticks. Whacker had been in charge then and for two months they'd strutted around the territory in their uniforms. It was exhilarating to be visually identifiable, instead of being just another kid. Everyone knew them as the Clockworks. They'd all been attracted by the violence of the gang that so resembled their own. The uniform wasn't a change of identity; it was basically only the donning of an elaborate mask. The mask isn't hideous and distorted, a monstrous creation of their imagining; but it is tragic in that the mask each one of them fits on is a perfect replica of his own face. The mask creates the illusion that Bicklo has changed character: he is the same boy and not created by *A Clockwork Orange,* even though onlookers might see in him and his spars the original of the film. Art is too often blamed for violence.

The foundations of Bicklo's violence had been carefully laid years ago. His mask is mere ritual. Like a bullfighter dressing in his suit of lights, the racing-driver donning his helmet, or a knight his armour, so Bicklo climbed into his Clockwork uniform. But it is really the final act of the play. His violence finds its origins in the concrete and asphalt womb in which he was born. Like a mother's womb it has undulated with the daily pressures, gradually distorting his vision, his thoughts, his actions. The act of violence on the screen or on the television is only a reflection of his own violence. His actions take place not after but before the film. *A Clockwork Orange* was only the imitation of his own life.

Bicklo ran into the flat and collected his jacket. He'd seen Paddy and Les and ran down to join them.

'What was Snowy doin'?' he asked as the three hurried to Warwick Street.

'Dunno,' Paddy said. 'He was runnin' somewhere la. When I called him he said "later".'

Bicklo wondered whether Snowy had found a screw. It must have been something to do with money, otherwise Snowy would never have run past Paddy. They caught the Shield Circular just in time. It was empty and they quickly made their way to the top and sat in front with their feet up against the rail. It was a 5p ride to Anfield, and within a mile the bus was completely packed. It roared past the long queues of men waiting and waving their scarves. Bicklo and his spars regally waved back. As the bus neared Anfield, the roads began to narrow. A great flood of people spilled over the pavements and moved steadily, like some giant river in full spate, towards the entrances of Liverpool Football Club's stadium. From high above, the pitch must have resembled a great green magnet magically sucking the vast flow of humans into its bowels. They came from all directions and half an hour before kick-off there was not an inch of asphalt to be seen for humans. The buses had stopped a mile away and the police horses sheltered against the wall. It was a good-natured, expectant, voluble crowd. The hum of conversation grew louder and louder until within the stadium walls it became a steady rumbling roar like water tumbling down a great fall.

Football is a part of the Liverpool charisma. Every man and boy in the city believes himself to be the greatest football fan in the country, the greatest authority on the game and the greatest player outside the two Liverpool teams. They psych the stranger into believing their self-made myth and finally psych each other. Football isn't a sport to the Liverpool fan. It is an obsession, a way of life to be followed from one end of the world to the other.

The game that day was between Stoke City and Liverpool. It was an emotional occasion. Gordon Banks, the great goalkeeper, was to make a farewell lap of honour. The great stand, the Kop, which was where Bicklo stood and which was famous for the spirit of its fans, had hated Banks at one time. In the first game he had ever played in Liverpool for Stoke he had saved so many goals that at the next match he had been pelted with rotten fruit, eggs and toilet rolls.

Bicklo was too young to remember that day. His mother had only allowed him to attend the games after he'd passed fourteen. She was well aware of the violence generated in the Kop. It came from the atmosphere, sucked in by the heat of a thousand bodies jammed in together, flesh pressed against flesh, the skin burning from the fire of another body, penetrating the flesh, the very personality and security of the other being until that moment of pure fear is reached. Only violence can clear a space; only violence can cut a swathe with fists and boots until the space to live and breathe is opened up again. Bicklo knew the Kop was always a place for sudden madness.

He and Paddy and Les pushed and shoved their way to a position behind the goal mouth and about halfway up the stands. They stood pressed against each other, unable to lift their arms. They scanned the faces to see if there was anyone familiar–a spar, a Dingle boy. Bicklo could see neither. He didn't expect ever to see a black face. There were actually one or two black fans, but they were standing at the very edge of the Kop, near the exit. Because of the potential for madness, no black kid ever attends the games. Marko and Ato knew they wouldn't survive a moment if Bicklo caught them in the crush. Yet the black kid's love for the game and his ability to play it, as he has often done for his school, is no less than the Boot Boy's. Fear keeps the black kids away and deprives them of their one chance to identify fully with the city of their birth; to be Liverpudlians, the greatest football supporters in the country. It is a brutal, savage piece of surgery that has torn this part of their inheritance from them. The wound forms the moment they become aware that they are so different that they cannot participate in this most common form of entertainment. It becomes bigger and calluses form around the edges as they grow older. At twenty they can attend the games unmolested, but by this time it is too late for them. The wound has congealed and hardened; apathy has set in. The voyage from the ghetto to Anfield is too long and the route has been forgotten.

Gordon Banks begins his lap of honour fifteen minutes before kick-off. He walks with his arms upraised like a victor, and bright electric emotion follows his every step. He stops the longest opposite Bicklo in the Kop. Bicklo curses him briefly for all those saves he never witnessed and then joins in to sing: 'Nice one, Gordon . . .'. They forget their past grudge, forgive him now that, half-blind, he leaves the game to lesser men. They are generous in their love for him; flooding him with their voices, wanting to touch him; for they know he won their grudging respect, the greatest fans in the country, by sheer greatness.

Before Banks can move on, a fight breaks out ten feet to the left of Bicklo. He can't see it; he is only aware that there's a fight because the wave of people clearing a space hits and pushes him back, crushes him even closer to Paddy and Les. 'C'mon!' Bicklo shouted. He pushed his way past the first tier of people. They now looked not towards Banks but towards the fight. It was beyond Bicklo's vision still even though he jumped and stood on tiptoe. The ripples of movement came from just beyond the heads and shoulders in front of him. Bicklo was driven by curiosity. He wanted to see who was battling; to be part of the danger that made the people clear a wide space. He wanted to join in if he knew the boys, or else egg the one on, hold the other. Banks moved on. The police were moving up from the ground but by the time they and Bicklo reached the fight it had finished. The battlers had dissolved into the crowd and the space filled as if nothing had happened. Bicklo turned back disappointed. He might even have known both the battlers. One a friend, the other an enemy. The game itself, after Banks and the fight, was an anticlimax. A goalless draw.

Trenchy was fucking bored. He and Gerald sat slouched very low in their 30p seats; their feet rested on the seats in front. Over the toes of his shoes, Trenchy could catch glimpses of the film. It was called *Man at the Top*. It was the additional feature and was a spin-off of a television series, which was the spin-off of a film which was the spin-off of a novel about a working-class man breaking the class barrier and making his way to the top. Trenchy didn't understand a single word of the film; he didn't recognise even one character. Joe Lampton, sleek and plump, driving a Rolls-Royce and talking in a working-class accent was pure s-h-i-t-e. Trenchy felt uneasily that he was being made fun of by this man who acted as if he were working-class. As for the upper-class people with their huge houses and fucking horses, they came from a different planet. Trenchy didn't even try to comprehend them. He couldn't believe they existed. He'd never seen them in real life, so he couldn't recognise them on the screen.

Trenchy wondered whether he should have gone to the game with Bicklo. He seldom attended football matches because of the battling. The madness turned him off. You could find yourself battling whether you liked it or not. The away games were the worst. In the train you'd sit down and a boy would say, 'That's my seat.' You moved to another. He'd repeat himself. It would go on for the whole length of the train until you battled.

Everybody in the cinema looked asleep and Trenchy yawned. It was taking hours to get to the Kung Fu picture. There was no one he recognised. On Sunday evenings there'd be hundreds. It was the roaring day when you came with your spars and your beef to shout and stomp and maybe even battle.

The Kung Fu film finally came on and Trenchy and Gerald cheered with the rest of the house. It passed in a smashing blur. Their guts kicked over with each chop, butt, smash, chop, chop. At the end they both nearly fell out of their seats as the hero chopped the villain's leg on the knee.

It was early evening when they came out. The weather had changed. The city was cloaked with a fine grey drizzle and the breeze coming in across the Mersey had a sharp bite. They buttoned their coats and cursed the weather. The huge Saturday afternoon shopping crowd had dried to a trickle of stragglers. It was only a five-minute walk to the bus stop in Renshaw Street but Trenchy and Gerald took fifteen minutes. They were re-enacting the Kung Fu film. Trenchy demonstrated the high kick while Gerald feinted with stiff-arm chops. They danced and circled each other in mock battle, not belonging to the streets of Liverpool but wholly wrapped in their imagination. Trenchy chased Gerald past the Wimpy bar. Neither saw the five black kids drifting up Ranelagh Street.

10

THEY were moving in a loose bunch. Three were trailing behind, stopping often to stare enviously into shop windows. The two in front were eating out of a single bag of chips which they passed back and forth. They saw Trenchy and Gerald first and stopped. They grinned at each other. Battling. They threw the bag of chips in the air, turned and sprinted down Ranelagh Street. The three other boys lifted their heads in question.

'Boot Boys. Two.'

The three swung in behind. They turned into Bold Street and jogged silently up the slope. The wet pavements glittered like mirrors under their feet and the windows caught their passing reflections. They all knew instinctively what action to take. If they came up behind Trenchy and Gerald, the white kids would run. By manœuvring up Bold Street and then cutting through Newington Street they would be able to confront the two head on. Steve and Carlos were leading.

Steve peeped around the corner of Renshaw Street. 'They're comin',' he whispered and stepped back.

Trenchy and Gerald were nearing their bus stop. The black kids scrabbled around for weapons. They found pop bottles, a brick and a chunk of wood.

'They've stopped at the fucking bus stop,' Carlos said in dismay. 'Bastards.' He was hurt by Trenchy and Gerald refusing to co-operate with his plan.

Trenchy and Gerald were breathing heavily. All that mock-battling was tiring and they leant against the wall to regain their breath and wait for the bus. There were four people in the queue. For the first time since leaving the cinema, Trenchy emerged from the fantasy and looked around. He knew it was a precaution he should have taken earlier. On weekends a lot of the fighting took place in the town centre. It was really guerilla warfare with boys making running attacks on each other. Sometimes it was the blacks, sometimes the Dingle and, if the football games were home games, an out of town gang. It made little difference if the town centre was packed with shoppers.

The first bus going to Prince's Park took two of the queue. Only two others were left with Trenchy and Gerald. Steve decided not to push his luck.

'Come on,' he said and walked casually into Renshaw Street. He held a bottle behind him and tried to stay as close to the buildings as possible. The others came up behind, in single file. They hadn't moved more than ten yards when Trenchy spotted them.

'Run,' he shouted, and took off down the slope back towards Lime Street. Gerald was a step behind. From far away came the crash of a breaking bottle. It had fallen far short of where they'd been standing and had been hurled more in frustration than with any intent to harm. Trenchy looked back as he neared Lewis's, Liverpool's largest department-store. Steve was leading the chase, running silently like some ancient hunter pacing himself to catch his game. The others were strung out behind him. Trenchy and Gerald cut up Bold Street, hoping the niggers wouldn't double back and try to cut them off. Trenchy slowed momentarily for Gerald to catch up. Carlos was now ahead of Steve and he paused to throw a bottle. It skidded, not breaking for a moment, until it hit the edge of the pavement. Trenchy flashed a V-sign and ran faster. Carlos ran smoothly. He was a whiplash boy, almost rubbery in all his movements, and he ran with a high knee lift. He'd been top sprinter in school and catching up with Trenchy was only a matter of a few more minutes. Trenchy and Gerald tried to accelerate. They were tiring and had stopped wasting energy trying to look back. They only had four more blocks to run before entering their territory and once inside they were safe. Not only because of their own gang but because Trenchy knew every inch like the back of his hand. He could disappear into a tenement and come out six streets further up; the black kids, though mad, would never be able to find him. A half-brick missed him by a yard and bounced on ahead of him. Instinctively he and Gerald began to weave in their run in case another was more accurate. The traffic on Duke Street, with the green light, was fast. Trenchy and Gerald didn't pause. They skipped and dodged among the cars, glimpsing the angry faces cursing them. Once in Suffolk Street, Trenchy slowed. He had reached safety. He looked back, thinking the niggers would have slowed down. They were cutting through the speeding cars with the same indifference as Trenchy and Gerald had, even stopping on the centre line to throw a hunk of wood that whirled far past them. Trenchy knew that on Great George Street, he'd find the others. He cut up Henry Street and into Kent, and looked back again. There was no sign of the niggers. He and Gerald slowed down to a walk. Their lungs were burning and both were covered with a film of fine sweat. It had been a long, hard run. The sharp, spiked heel of fear had given them breath, lent them speed and wit. If they'd panicked or tired, they both knew they would have been given a terrible battering. The niggers were merciless, so they'd been told. They'd heard stories of niggers even beating up your beef if you were caught by them with her. No Boot Boy ever did that. His battling was done with boys, not beef. The niggers would also batter you to unconsciousness and still keep on. The Boot Boy just gave you a good fair battering to teach you a lesson and left you alone. The Boot Boy, as seen by himself, was the protector of women, a respecter of their frailty, an upholder of the rules of knightly battle. The niggers were none of these things. Of course, the black kids said the same about the honky trash–beef-beaters, sadists.

Like miniature nations, they fed themselves and the other side with rumours and propaganda. They gorged themselves on mere words which were passed from one to another and gave them strength. There had been efforts to bring down the barriers each side had constructed. Bill Harp, the leader of the Great George's project, once filmed the black kids on video discussing the problems of the Boot Boys. He ran this for the Boot Boys and tried to get them to discuss their side of the problem, but they refused and the idea had failed. Even if it had succeeded, the confrontation in the flesh, rather than through their video images, would have not worked. It seldom did. When the Blackie closed for decorations, the black kids had been invited to use the Yorkie. The youth workers hoped that by fraternisation the tension would be eased; maybe even erased. The first day, it had been like sitting on a volcano; on the second day the volcano erupted. The fighting had started over beef: the initial battling always started over beef. In a shadow imitation of some primeval society, the two gangs would fight over women, usually white women. They'd battled in Rank's dance-hall, until Rank's tried to limit the number of blacks they would allow in. Accused of racial discrimination they changed the policy but the Boot Boys kept dropping out because they couldn't stand the competition for their beef.

The black kids with their mythical pricks, their sharp clothes, their rhythm, and finally the beauty of their half-caste faces and bodies, were beyond the reach of the Boot Boys. A few of the white kids had the style of the blacks, but in spite of themselves it always seemed only in imitation. Never original, for they lacked the edge of arrogance the black man has. In the dance-halls and clubs the Boot Boy would watch with envy as the best beef in the hall were taken by the black kids. Each black kid's beef was better than the one he had. He couldn't help this. His vision was distorted by jealousy; in his rage he attributed beauty to the white girl's face and body. He may call her a nigger-lover but he knows at last that somehow he has been defeated. He's been rejected for this black boy. The girl, in her choice of the black boy, has given him an additional potency, some further magic that makes him more attractive to the other white girls. In a society where the woman is a possession, this theft of one more material object enraged the Boot Boy further. It made him fight harder, not so much for the woman but to prove that he had enough 'wealth' with which to own the woman. It wasn't the gang beef that worried the Boot Boy, for though they belonged to no one in particular and always hung around the gang they always had fidelity. It was the floaters, the strangers who'd show up at the dance-halls and clubs. The ones the Boot Boys wanted the most, and they were the beef who'd walk with a black kid. The sexual battling reached far deeper into their psyche than did the battling over territory: it was their race battling.

Trenchy and Gerald, once they had entered their territory, believed themselves safe. They slowed to a walk, more a saunter of victory for they'd just survived another battle (it became a battle once they began to relate it to the others). They were near the car showrooms, not more than a hundred yards from the Yorkie when a half-brick shattered a foot from Trenchy. Instinctively, they both ran. Coming towards them at a dead run, like the cavalry to the rescue, were Bicklo, Snowy, Pat and half a dozen others.

'Kill the niggers,' Bicklo shouted. He picked up a brick and threw it back. Cars stopped on either side of the cleared space where the bricks and bottles bounced and skidded towards each other. They 'fought' for fifteen minutes until, as they slowly grew bored of repeated near-misses, the two sides drifted apart. The light was fading, the road was a mess of splintered glass and bricks and wood, it was time for tea. Bicklo stayed on a few minutes longer while Trenchy drifted home with Gerald. He wouldn't mention the chase to his parents as they hated his getting involved in any of the fighting. It was Saturday evening and his father would be in the pub having a few pints while his mother, once she had made tea, would be dressing up for the weekly outing to the Lewis's club dance. It was a Saturday ritual Trenchy's parents tried never to miss, and Trenchy, rather than prowl the streets as the other kids would do, preferred to watch television until they returned home. It was the ending of his day as he went home.

Bicklo lingered with Snowy and Paul. They sat on the railings all facing the same way–down Upper Pitt Street with their backs to Great George Street. There was little to see and the drizzle was gradually turning to rain. Cars flashed by on Great George Street. It was as if they'd turned their backs on the world. They were quiet for a long time. Their hunched shoulders reflected a mood of sadness, an almost limitless exhaustion with the world. The burden of living they had found already to be almost unbearable. The day was slipping through their wide-spread fingers like a thick, slow treacle dripping to the ground. Their collective imaginations had come to a dead end. It wasn't the lack of money that made the evening to come look so long and tedious. It was the lack of a dream, of the ability to visualise a limitless world beyond the borders of their territory. The dreams had been lost in the distant past of childhood; removed from them even at the moment of birth. There was so little chance for dreams in a crowded flat in a tenement on the banks of the Mersey. They were snatched from them by the scream of parents, the crying of their brothers and sisters, the need to hunt at an early age. Like Stone Age children they'd learnt to survive too early in life. And as the child grew older his imagination, his chance to dream grew less, shredded and sliced to pieces by the pressures of the tenement. It diminished him like some slow-burning, guttering candle until all that was left was a human form sitting on a railing staring at an empty street.

'Fucking rain,' Bicklo said.

No one answered. He wiped his face and flicked the drops into the air. He couldn't think of anything to do. If Whacker had been there. . . . Bicklo pushed the thought out of his mind.

'I feel like a drink la,' he suggested. Again there was silence. 'I mean not buyin' la. We'll screw that restaurant I told you about.'

'I need a drink,' Snowy said. 'A free whisky. It would taste good la. We'll do it after tea.'

For these three the day hadn't been good and even the thought of the screw didn't cheer them up. What promise there had been at the start had slipped away unfulfilled. Snowy took a deep breath and blew out. It sounded so final, like a man who faced complete defeat.

'What shall I do la?' he finally asked. His face was twisted into concentration and regret. He spat.

'Phone her,' Bicklo said non-committally.

'But what can I tell her la?' Snowy said. 'I promised to see her today and I can't get any fucking bread.'

'You broke your leg,' Paul suggested and grinned.

Snowy pushed him. 'Fuck off. I told her last time me brother broke his arm. If I say I broke me leg she'll think what funny people live in Liverpool la. They keep breaking arms, legs just as they're coming to visit me.'

'Tell her you don't have the bread,' Bicklo said.

'Tell her you found better pussy here,' Paul said.

'If only I could. All the fuckfaces here have sour pussies la. Like their fucking faces. No la, this pussy in Blackpool is so sweet. I swear she really loves me la. I can feel it when she talks on the phone. Her voice. . . .' He sighed and kept yearning for her. Maybe he would phone later, if he could think up a good excuse. Though lack of money was the truth, he didn't want her to know that he was so fucking useless that he couldn't raise enough bread to get up to Blackpool. For fuck's sake, what would she think of him?

'Who squealed, then?' Paul asked the question generally. Both Bicklo and Snowy shrugged.

'I should have done that la,' Snowy said brightly. 'If I'd squealed on that camera I'd have fifty sheets now la. A new suit, shoes and first-class to Blackpool. Dinner in some posh place. Can you see me la in one of those expensive Chinese places, with a bill for five sheets and taking out a fat roll. I swear that pussy's eyes would pop.' He stopped for a moment and then said contritely: 'I did think of it, not that I would have squealed. I need the bread but not that bad.'

At five, the panic over the camera had ended. By the time Bicklo returned from a wasted afternoon watching bad football, someone had squealed and Pete, the boy who'd screwed the car, had been picked up by the pigs. According to rumour–no one was going to go up and ask the pigs or the boy's family questions–the pigs had known exactly where to look. They'd arrived at the flat with a search warrant, which meant they were sure it was in the flat, and had gone straight to the clothes cupboard, knelt and turned over the pile of dirty linen.

'Must have been his brother,' Bicklo guessed, 'or maybe his dad.'

'Could be la,' Paul said. 'How else would the pigs know exactly where to look. None of us knew it was in the clothes cupboard,' forgetting everyone knew.

'He's a bloody fool, anyway,' Snowy pronounced after a moment's thought.

'I mean, he knew the camera was really hot la. If I was him I'd have hidden it ... somewhere else. Don't ask me where. Somewhere. Not in the fucking flat.'

'Four ... thousand ... sheets,' Bicklo said in an awed whisper.

'I wonder what it looks like,' Paul said. 'In a pile, I mean.'

'We'd be fucking millionaires,' Snowy said. 'Four thousand la. And here when we have twenty sheets on us we think we're fucking rich.'

They fell silent. Each trying to visualise that vast amount of money all in one pile which, they felt, would no doubt rise up to the sky. Four thousand! It was an infinite, inexhaustible sum of cash. They could see it stretching out and lasting until the end of their lives, wrapping them in the warmth of affluence. They could just about imagine it. Though never wholly, for they didn't know what they could do with the money. Buy a car, yes. Beyond that they were vague. They did know it would relieve the pressure of physically scrambling for money–working, screwing, hustling. It would add a grace to their lives, a finish to their skin, their accents, their hair, their whole bodies. Like a gloss-paint job on rough metal. It would have been a magic garb, composed of crisp paper, to have grabbed and donned and then floated across the hard pavements of Liverpool 8.

'I'm going back for me tea,' Bicklo said at last and slid off the railing.

'Later la,' Snowy said and set off up Upper Pitt Street.

'Later,' Paul said and went up Great George.

Bicklo set off at his usual trot. He shook his head. Four thousand sheets. It made him feel sick in the stomach that there was so much money to spend on something like a fucking camera. They should have given it to him.

119

Marko too daydreamed of money. Not of cash but of the perfect screw. He dreamt, as he walked up to Windsor Street, of this screw where the safe was loaded with money and wide open; where the T.V.s, the radios, the tapes lay on the shelf. Glittering like jewels in a vault and ready for the taking by the conqueror who entered. No pigs to hustle you. You just walked in and walked out with your arms loaded.

Marko had a pound fifty in his pocket, which he would spend mostly on drag. It was the weekend and a time to enjoy oneself, though for the most part he was a frugal boy. The clothes he was wearing were his best, and the same as he'd worn in the morning. Cord trousers, a turtle-neck pullover and a leather jacket. It was what he wore every Friday and Saturday night. He didn't believe in spending too much on gear. If he did decide to go mad and spend money, it would be on sounds. 'Alan,' he shouted when he reached Windsor and stood in front of the council block. 'Alan!'

Alan opened the window and stuck his head out. Marko sheltered in the hall. It always seemed that his life had stuck in the same pattern. He would catch a sudden glimpse of himself, dressed the same, thinking the same, doing the same things. Always waiting for something to happen. He knew that was how the rest of the evening was going to be, like the evening before that, and the evening before that. Always the same evening repeating itself. Waiting for things to happen. He, like Bicklo and Ato and Trenchy and all the others, was incapable of initiating anything himself. This was the beginning of the waiting: when Alan shot out of the block the two drifted side by side into the ghetto. It was seven and the rain looked yellow against the lighted windows. Marko stopped once he'd crossed into the ghetto and rolled a joint. It was his last lump of drag and he softened it extra-carefully and spread it out over the cigarette paper. Having rolled it, he searched in his hair for a match. He thought he had one there but after poking around in his Afro he dropped the stick into his coat pocket.

Alan talked non-stop, but Marko was silent and only answered in grunts or threw out a 'True . . . true' as some placatory morsel to his friend. Alan's chatter, mostly malicious gossip, didn't interest him and he was still dreaming of finding an Aladdin's cave to screw. They reached Upper Stanhope Street. It was empty of adults but populated with kids. They were standing around in knots or drifting between the chippies and the Pony Express café. Alan split for chips and Marko moved on to the Pony Express. It

120

was packed with kids, mostly playing the pinball or the fruit machine. Ato sipped a coke and wandered around the café somewhat lost. He felt zombie-like and was still worrying about the lice in his place. He knew it would take him years to get rid of his phobia.

'Whacha doin' la?' Marko asked.

Ato shrugged. 'Hear there's a shebeen later, man. Don' know where but we'll find it.'

Marko took a matchbox from one of the kids.

'None of that shit here,' Akhmed shouted from behind the counter. 'You want to smoke your poison, do it elsewhere. No here. The cops will. . . .'

'Keep your hair on,' Marko said and put away the stick. He sat down at the table without ordering anything. Few of the kids bought anything. They would play the machines until they ran out of change and then drift out.

Saturdays were particularly dull. None of the youth clubs were open so you couldn't start the evening there. During the week when they were open you could start off at the Blackie–it gave you some sort of impetus–almost like winding up the motor–and then move on to other action. Without the wind-up, Saturday took a very long time to take on any shape, if it ever did.

'Want to play cards?' Marko asked generally. Three or four, including Ato, agreed to a 'quick' game. They always thought it would be quick for there'd be something for sure for them to do halfway through the game; and usually the game went on for hours as they waited. The game was going to be held on the same stair-level as every other night, and in the same building. While the others wandered over, Marko ducked into Cliff's wine-store, two shop-fronts away from the Pony Express. He needed cigarettes to make up his joints. Cliff Cole was a young, light-skinned half-caste. A handsome, slim man with a neatly clipped moustache. He'd owned Cliff's wine-store, the only liquor-shop in the ghetto, for the last two years. One shop away was his wife's business, Irene's hairdressing salon. Irene, pretty and efficient, was a few years younger than Cliff. She owned the only salon in Liverpool that specialised in black people's hair, and had a booming business. Both Cliff and Irene claimed the longest history of Black Liverpudlians. Irene went back to her great-grandfather settling in Liverpool in the nineteenth century; Cliff claimed a grandfather in the early twentieth century. They were both the scions of old-established black families. They had the tradition of the white middle class–a work-success ethic handed down over two generations that made them both stay at their businesses until late at night. Irene's mother was the owner of the Gladray nightclub about half a mile up Upper Parliament Street.

Their financial and business success had prompted them to move away from the ghetto and they'd bought a house in Aigburth, a residential district a few miles to the east. But they weren't very happy there. The families surrounding them were all white, and both Cliff and Irene felt the discrimination. Because of this, they were vaguely planning to return to the ghetto; to live once more among their own people, to be one of a kind, rather than an isolated black couple living in a middle-class suburb. The pressure to return to this 'homeland', in spite of their confidence, their success and their financial strength, was gradually increasing. They both knew, also, that this return would trap them and their children in the ghetto mentality. They could, through their ambition and maturity, combat its sapping effect. The two children, however, would have none of that strength. Like Marko, they would take to the streets–the card-games, the thieving, the fighting. In Aigburth, at least, isolated by their colour, they obeyed their parents. The Coles hadn't yet made up their minds, though they often talked about the moves and counter-moves of their future.

Marko took about fifteen minutes to get to the card-game. It wasn't more than a block away but he had some business to attend to. A taxi-driver on Berkeley Street had found a house worth screwing and gave Marko a pound as an advance for the job. It was routine. A cab-driver, dropping off a drunk or a woman, knew when a house was left unoccupied; he cased it and had one of the kids screw the place for him. If the kid was gripped, he wouldn't squeal to the pigs. It was a selfish, destructive arrangement but Marko could only see the immediate cash gain. He was also flattered to be used by one of the 'big' boys, to be entrusted with such a delicate mission. To him, it was a sure sign that the boys thought him a smart kid, a clever boy who would go far in life. If not, why did they give him these jobs? They knew that if he didn't do it for them he'd do it for someone else. Or for himself. Marko's corruption was well known in the ghetto, like a few other black kids'. The big boys knew who'd do a screw, smoke drag, pinch a car. The corruption was there on the open counter and Marko had chosen. From his schooldays he'd been doing screws, and each time he was caught the headmaster had let him off with a warning. The warnings had accumulated in his young life, until he came to the conclusion that his life was to be only filled with warnings. The authorities were fools, and he, Marko, a smart boy, gifted by God to escape the penalties of his crimes, was going to continue fooling them. Marko lived in his fantasies more securely, more warmly, than any other kid in the ghetto. What was worse, he wouldn't believe that his life was a fantasy. Unlike Ato, who made an effort to separate reality and fantasy, Marko cast his fantasies as reality. Phil Cantor, Sue Shaffer, Bobby Nyahoe and many others who liked Marko, and those who had no affection–the pigs and the magistrates–would warn him of his coming destruction. He wouldn't believe them. He just couldn't see how this idyll could ever come to an end. He'd nod at each warning and lecture and say wisely, 'True . . . true . . .'. He never believed any of it for a moment. He was too smart to get caught; he believed this in spite of his own lengthening record. Only three days ago, he'd been gripped by the pigs walking down Parly at two in the morning carrying a car battery. A car battery! When the pigs asked him where the battery had come from, Marko said, 'My car's stalled up the road.' They made him take them to the car, and gripped him. His hearing was a month away and he knew they'd let him off with a warning.

At times, Marko would know his life could have been different. But this knowledge was faint, a sounding from the deep, far distant centres in his brain. A warning rising from the depths which in no way altered his course. At these times, when a vague unease entered him, he wished for his father, the unknown man who had sired him and whom he'd never once seen. At these times he would want to make the journey to London, maybe even further to Africa to find this man and ask him to take care of him. If he had followed that urge in the first place, Marko knew he too could have been a doctor, like his father. Maybe his father was a doctor, maybe even a surgeon. Marko wasn't sure. He believed his father to belong to the most stable of professions, a doctor. And he could have been Dr Ivor Markham. Instead he was Marko. The name, so stunted, reflected his status–a half-caste ghetto-kid.

He was feeling very cheerful as he ambled towards the card game. He had a 'job' and a sheet had found its way into his pocket. It was by keeping his eyes wide open, by playing smart that the sheet lay in his pocket. There were nearly eight kids on the halfway landing grouped around a pile of small change on the floor with their First Call cards in their hands. Marko hoisted himself onto the sill of the glassless window and watched. The game finished quickly as Brian called almost immediately. Marko threw down his money and whistled tunelessly to himself.

'I've found something out,' Ato announced from his cards. He was secretly pleased. He'd heard there was to be a shebeen in a house off Granby Street.

'What?' Marko asked.

'Later la later. Too many ears to listen here. Right?'

'True,' Marko said.

'You found a shebeen, have you?' Alan asked.

'You've got a big mouth Alan la,' Ato said and sulkily looked down at his cards. It had been his little secret. A shebeen, however, in the ghetto, was no one's secret. Within a few minutes of its being announced everyone knew. They were meant to. The more people the better. The louder the music, the more the money, the more the booze, the more the pot. It would be really, really hot. A good hot shebeen. They'd run for two days at a time. And close down on the third. The reason was simple. If the pigs found the shebeen, they had to watch the premises for two days before a warrant could be issued. Ato was looking forward to it. Anticipation was almost a sensual pleasure and he would put off going until maybe two in the morning, when all the good anticipation, when he was feeling full of power, would explode in the shebeen. He'd dance la. A real power-dance and everyone would stand by and watch him and applaud at the end. Ato was a very good dancer. High on drag, he knew he would be even better.

11

IT was raining and cold. Occasionally, a strong gust of wind would blow the rain through the open hallway and drench the sheltering boys. There were twenty-five of them watching the wind make the rain dart back and forth across Great George Street. Bicklo sat on the top stair with Snowy and Paul; the others were grouped below him. A few sat on the cold floor with their backs to the walls. If it had been dry they would all have been sitting on the railings a few yards away.

'There's Beno la,' Snowy said. 'With Trevor. Beno!'

They all shouted the names and Beno and Trevor ran into the hallway. Their jackets were dark with rain and their bellbottoms soggy. Beno carefully wiped water off his hair and face.

'You goin' to the Cabaret, then?' Bicklo asked unnecessarily. It was a disco on Duke Street frequented by the Boot Boys, and ties and jackets were compulsory.

'Found five sheets,' Beno said with a grin. He pulled out the notes and flourished them as proof of his affluence. Beno lived on the dole. He'd been trying for a job for nearly a year now and had given up expecting one. His life consisted entirely of waiting for Thursdays. Thursday was dole day, and once it was over and he'd received his money there was little else to do. Sometimes he'd be lucky enough to find the odd fiver, which he'd spend every Saturday in the Cabaret. 'Anyone else goin'?' he asked.

Everyone shook their heads. Nobody had the money for the entrance. Beno shook his head in mock sympathy and carefully tucked the money back into his pockets. He pushed his way up the stairs to sit behind Bicklo. He wasn't in a hurry to make the Cabaret. The action only started at ten. He glanced at his watch. Another hour to go. He wished the rain would stop soon; it was over a mile to the Cabaret and by the time they reached it he'd be soaked to the skin.

'I wish Swingles was open,' Snowy said. 'It was a great place la. We really had some fun there.'

'Fuckin' great place,' Bicklo said. They all agreed with him.

'We'd still have it if it weren't for the fuckin' Fire Brigade. Slow bastards.'

Swingles had been their favourite youth club. It had been a thousand times better than the Yorkie. It had had a fabulous disco, a new gym, any number of games, concerts, coffee bar, snack bar. Everything that they'd ever wanted. They'd burnt it down one winter evening. Not that they meant to. Whacker had decided to make a raid on the Blackie with petrol bombs. For two days they'd all conspired at making up half a dozen bombs. Whacker knew how to make them. He'd heard from his father's friend. The following night four of them had set out to make the attack. On the way they decided to test the bombs. They'd look fools if they threw dud bottles into the Blackie. They decided to test just one of them. The rest were reserved for the attack on the Blackie. Swingles had a wall with a high window. They lit one bomb and threw it against the wall. It exploded in a marvellous bloom of orange fire. It was so beautiful to look at that they decided to use just one more. They lit it and threw it hurriedly. The bomb went right through the window and exploded inside Swingles. Within a few minutes the whole building was alight. It was really ace the way the place burnt. It was too late now for them to attack the Blackie, and the bombs were powerful evidence against them. They threw the remaining four through the windows and called the Fire Brigade.

They'd watched it burn from a distance. The night for a brief while looked like a waning day. They felt sad as Swingles slowly folded, broke and blackened. The firemen could do nothing. They really hadn't meant to burn Swingles. The moment had trapped them and swept them blindly on to destruction. They'd been unable to control their excitement, their exhilaration at watching the beautiful flames leap and dance and consume. It had just happened too quickly, and when it was all over they'd crept down to watch the dark, heavy smoke twist and drift in the night breeze. They'd wandered around it for an hour, watching its death with the puzzled emptiness of wolves circling a dying comrade. It looked as helpless and joyless as they did. When it was safe to pick through the cooling brick and wood, they entered and removed the copper. Copper had a good price.

They talked about Swingles and the good times they'd had.

Cursing the Fire Brigade for not having won the battle and saved them from their own destruction.

'Get out of the way,' a man said loudly.

They all looked up. On the half-landing a middle-aged man and his wife were impatiently hovering. It was the Croxleys, Jimmy's parents. Mr Croxley was always angry with them and without waiting he began descending. He stepped on Beno's jacket and would have put his foot on Snowy's hand, if Snowy hadn't jumped.

'Don't you have anything else to do except sit around here?' Mrs Croxley demanded as she followed her husband. 'Nothing but layabouts.'

'Come on,' Croxley said, 'get out of here–all of you. Otherwise I'll call the police.' He stood at the bottom and kept jerking his head to the exit.

One by one they slowly rose and hesitantly drifted out. The rain had eased just slightly, and they clung to the sides of the council house to gain what little shelter they could. Mr Croxley waited until they'd all vacated the hallway before buttoning his raincoat and taking his wife's arm.

'They're the ones who cause all the trouble,' he said as they set off down Upper Pitt Street. 'In my day. . . .' They moved out of hearing distance and the boys drifted back to the hallway.

Bicklo and Snowy waited until the rain had become a fine drizzle. They looked at each other and nodded.

'Later la,' they said and moved out of the hallway. They looked around and set off to Nelson Street. Snowy had sussed the Chink restaurant out an hour earlier. It had been closed now for over a month and nobody guarded the premises. The rain had kept the streets empty, and apart from one or two couples moving off to pubs they had the streets to themselves. It was an easy screw. Snowy shoved his heel hard against the basement door and the lock splintered and broke. They groped their way up the stairs. It was a dusty, damp building. Silent and ghostlike. The tables and chairs were stacked neatly against the walls as if it had closed only for the night. The bar was near the front window. Snowy ducked as he crossed the patch of light and scuttled behind the bar. He reached up and took down five bottles–two of scotch, one of gin, one vodka and one brandy. He hated brandy and threw the bottle into the bin as they made their way out. Luckily it didn't break or make a noise.

Carrying two bottles each, they ran back to the railings. As it was only spitting the boys had come to sit outside. Snowy opened the bottle of scotch and took a mouthful. He spat it out.

'Awful la,' he swore. 'I don't know how people drink this shite.' He then tried the gin and the vodka. On each he passed the same opinion.

'Mix it with coke la,' Paddy suggested after he had tasted it. 'It'll taste better. Not as good as beer though.'

Snowy bought a large bottle of coke from the Chinese chippy in front of the Blackie and they poured out half the contents from each bottle and topped them up with coke. They agreed it tasted better with coke and passed the bottles around. Beno and Trevor took a last mouthful each and left for the Cabaret.

Snowy collected the half-empty bottles and with Bicklo and Paddy went to the Yorkie. They tried the front door in the forlorn hope it would be open. It was shut. Bicklo cut round to the back while Snowy and Paddy sat on the steps to wait. On the west side of the Yorkie a drainpipe ran straight up past the gym window. Bicklo gripped and pulled himself up slowly, resting at each ledge for a minute or two to allow his arm muscles to relax. It was a three-storey climb and by the time he reached the window he felt exhausted. The window was closed. Holding on to the pipe with one hand, with his toes tucked into a niche, Bicklo opened the window. It wasn't very big. It just about fitted his shoulders as he wriggled through head first. On the other side was a ten-foot drop to the wooden floor. Bicklo twisted around painfully. He had to manoeuvre his legs through while he clung to the windowsill. As he'd done the feat often, it wasn't all that difficult. But it took time and care. He let go and dropped and rolled.

It was pitch black in the gym. The window was too high to give any light and, though he waited, his eyes didn't adjust. He couldn't even see his hand in front of him. He reached out and touched the cool wall. Keeping the wall as a guide he moved quickly across the empty gym to the stairs. He knew every inch of the building and automatically adjusted his step for the first stair. He ran down, with his hands sliding down the iron banister. The front door had four heavy iron bolts. The Settlement locked the door from the inside and then locked the passage connecting the two buildings. Locks on the outside were easily smashed.

Snowy and Paddy quickly slipped in and Bicklo locked the door behind them. They stood together for a moment in the blackness and felt calm. It was as if they'd finally returned to the only shelter they ever knew. Bicklo started up the stairs and Paddy followed. Snowy stayed where he was.

'You got a torch la,' he called up plaintively.

'What for?' Bicklo called back.

'I don't like the dark.'

Paddy only had matches and he lit one. As they climbed the weak yellow flame made the blurred shadows shift and jump. It seemed as if they were walking through a subterranean cave far from the surface of the world. The scribbles on the bare walls took on intricate shapes and patterns as the shadows brushed past them. They looked, briefly, like those ancient, innocent drawings sketched by long-forgotten men, and the messages they conveyed were in a code that only they understood and no outside man would ever be able to decipher. There were pools of water on the floor below the windows and here and there where the floor sloped long, thin rivulets snaked over the stairs to fall steadily into the black basement far below.

The three boys made their way to the small room that was off the gym. The mattresses near the window were soaked. They piled three or four dry ones near the door and lay back on them. Though the window was wide open and the wind cold, the room generated a strange warmth. It was as cosy as a dry cave hidden in the depth of a mountain. They lit cigarettes and sipped the booze and whispered.

'We goin' to stay here till one?' Snowy asked.

'What else to do?' Paddy asked.

'Must be something,' Bicklo said. 'Maybe I can catch some pussy before one.'

'There'll only be fuckfaces round now,' Snowy said. 'The best stuff comes out at one.'

'I'm goin' to get some pussy tonight,' Bicklo said. 'I can feel it in my prick.' They all laughed and talked about the pussy they'd soon be having. Snowy wasn't enthusiastic. Nothing would ever compare to his Blackpool beef. Her memory was still fresh and he didn't want to soil it with some sour fuckface.

After fifteen minutes they started to get restless and Bicklo began to prowl to the window and back again. Nile Street always looked empty. It was what lay beyond that tempted him. There must be something happening on Great George Street or Duke Street or. . . . Finally he could take it no longer.

'I'm goin' out,' he announced and left the room.

129

Paddy automatically rose and followed. Snowy did the same, after tucking the bottles under a mattress.

'Why don't you stay,' Bicklo said as they went down the stairs.

'Too fuckin' dark for me la,' Snowy said.

They closed the door behind them, jamming a wad of paper to keep it from swinging open. The cobbled street shone dully from the far-off street-lamp. The drizzle had finally stopped and the sky was so clear that they could see the stars and a faint moon. Not that they looked up as they hurried down Nile Street.

Marko sat on the parapet and waited for Ato to pass him the joint. They were both feeling good. The card-game was still going on half a floor above them. They'd won 40p each and had decided to quit while they were ahead. Robbie came to join them and to share the joint. Like the night before the square was full of kids running messages, chasing each other, rapping. The pubs had just closed and a few of the older people, swaying and talking loudly, passed on their way home or to a club for some further drinking.

'When'll we go to the shebeen la?' Ato asked.

Marko shrugged. He wasn't sure whether he wanted to attend it. There was the possibility of some more interesting action that night. He hoped it would materialise.

'We'll make it la,' Ato suggested. 'Two . . . three. That's the best time la. The music's hot and it will be full of people all feelin' good.' He laughed and experimented with a few dance steps. His legs were aching for action.

Suddenly there was a loud shout from the flat behind them. None of them paid any attention as a man's voice rose and fell in anguish. He was shouting at somebody or something and it was none of their concern. The man moved out of the flat and they could hear him shouting louder. He was coming nearer and straight towards them. They tensed. He was hunting for them and suddenly the voice was no longer just loud. They could feel the rage in every word.

The man who took the corner looked angry and nervous. He was white, middle-aged, and dressed in a suit. His shirt was open down to his belly, his hair was straight and fell slightly over his forehead. His face looked like one of those strangely shaped potatoes–a large, bumpy nose and a pouting chin. A step behind him came his wife. She was short and slim and looked even more nervous than he did.

There was so much tension in her face that one wasn't sure whether she was going to cry or just collapse or scream.

'You're the ones who did it,' George Macken said. He jabbed a finger in the general direction of Marko, Ato and Robbie.

'Did what la?' Robbie asked slowly and carefully. He sat loosely on the parapet next to Marko. Ato just leaned against the wall and folded his arms, while Marko stared straight ahead lost in very deep thought.

'I and my missus just got back from the pub. Somebody broke into the flat and stole my telly.' George was trying to speak slowly but the anger and nervousness pushed the words out faster and faster. 'One of you did it. You're always hanging round here and you seen us go out.'

'Hold it,' Robbie said. He lost his casualness and the edge of anger entered his voice. 'You can't just go round saying "You did it." We've done nothing. We've just been sitting here rapping.'

'All the time?' George asked softly.

'Yah. So fuck off.'

'Then you must have heard the break in,' he said triumphantly. 'They kicked my front door in. You must have heard it.'

'I heard nothing,' Robbie said.

'You half-caste kids are just scum,' Patsy Macken suddenly screamed.

'You've been pressuring us for a year now. Well, you've got your wish: we're leaving this stinking ghetto. You've been banging on our walls at all times of night, you've broken our windows, you've threatened my children. I've had enough of you all. I'm sick of you.'

'You can get the fuck out,' Robbie shouted, 'but don't call us black bastards.'

'I never did.'

'You did. I heard you.' Robbie became so excited that he nearly pushed Patsy down. In her rage Patsy couldn't remember what she'd said, and in his rage Robbie was sure she'd called him a bastard.

'She didn't,' George said. 'I heard what she said. Look, mate, you can't accuse us of colour prejudice. We were the first family to move into this block and nearly all my friends are coloured. For Christ's sake, I've got coloured nephews. She didn't call you a black bastard. Patsy never would.' George had managed to calm himself. He wanted desperately to explain to Robbie. To tell him his rage wasn't because of colour but because of the constant attacks on him and his family. But somehow it all was getting jumbled up. They weren't talking about his television set any more. They were fighting a racial battle with words and George was being forced to stand on a ground he'd never stood on before.

'Look, I fucking heard her,' Robbie said angrily. He turned to Marko and Ato and a dozen other kids who'd suddenly materialised. 'Right la.'

'I heard her,' Ato said.

'You're a bloody liar,' George said. He suddenly seemed to wilt and his shoulders sagged. He knew he was losing. They were going around in circles and he was standing in the centre slowly going mad. He was sure he was mad. He'd lived in the block for ten years and suddenly everyone was hating him. He was sure he'd done nothing wrong, but yet they were all standing around accusing him. He just wanted peace. For the last year the kids had really put on the pressure. It had reached the stage where he'd lost his job as an ambulance driver because it was night work and his wife had insisted he remain at home and protect the children. They'd been begging the Housing Department to move them. Day in and day out, and nothing happened. He took Patsy's arm gently and they turned away from the kids. Patsy looked back over her shoulder.

'Why are you attacking us?' she asked. She was puzzled and had been yearning to ask that question for long months. 'We've done you no harm.'

Robbie smiled very gently. 'You've got to understand la. Who else can we attack? The pigs, and the Government, we can't reach them. That leaves you. People on the streets whom we can reach and get our revenge.'

Patsy didn't understand. She shook her head as if trying to clear it. Words, words. Such puzzles in all those words.

'But you're white like me,' George suddenly noticed.

Robbie looked down at the skin on his bare arm and studied it as if he were seeing it for the first time. George Macken was right. But Robbie shook his head.

'I don't see no white skin la. It's black.'

'It's white,' George insisted. He came to stand next to Robbie and bared his arm to compare the two skins. Robbie pulled back quickly.

'It's black,' he insisted angrily. He pointed to his head.

'It's black in there as well.'

'You're mad,' Patsy said. 'You're white and you say you're black.'

'Don't call me mad,' Robbie screamed. '*You* are la. I'm white now, but when I come and ask you for a job I'll suddenly become black. Don't you think I don't know your tricks. I've learnt everything you can teach me and', Robbie spat slowly, 'I am a black man.'

George and Patsy walked slowly away down the passage. Patsy was crying silently and George held her arm and squeezed. He looked around helplessly. No one moved. The kids watched them silently, until they turned the corner to their flat. The pain never stops.

'Who did it la?' Robbie asked generally. Everyone shrugged and the kids drifted away. 'Shite. He made me so mad. I'm goin' to the Pun. I need sounds, loud sounds to make me feel better.'

'I'll come', Ato said. 'Marko?'

Marko was still staring into the distance. He shook his head.

'I got business la,' he said. 'Big business.'

Eight of them moved slowly, aimlessly up Great George Street. Bicklo and Snowy were in front, behind were Paddy, Steve, Dee, Jean and Mary. Bill was on the other side of the street rapping. Dee had wanted to buy chips, so everyone moved along with her. It was better than hanging round the railings.

Dee had just come out of the chippy when the fighting broke out. It started in the Chinese restaurant ten yards from where they were standing. It broke on to the street with five men falling and tumbling over each other. Two were Chinese, three were dockers. Bicklo and the kids ran towards the fight. One docker had a Chink against the car and in awful slow motion was punching him in the belly, the other two had the second Chink on the floor. They were kicking him. Bicklo cheered them on. The violence was magnetic. The kids edged closer and closer, as if wanting to study every punch and counterpunch. Jean got too close. She was a thin, solemn girl who never smiled. She seldom spoke either and there was an almost doll-like frailty to her. A big Chink, holding a stool, ran out of the restaurant and began hitting one of the dockers around the head and shoulders. He finally swung hard and missed. The stool slipped out of his hand and slammed into Jean's wrist before bouncing on to a parked car.

'Oh my god,' she screamed. She clutched her hand and slowly folded down onto the pavement. The boys ran to her and half-lifted and carried her across the road. They examined the hand under a streetlamp, completely forgetting about the fighting.

'It's broken la,' Bicklo said. He studied Jean. He had expected her to be crying, but though she was in pain her face looked stubborn. It looked as if she'd made up her mind a long time ago that she would never ever cry.

Snowy unwrapped the ragged bandage off his hand and slowly wound it round Jean's. He didn't do a very good job, as she wasn't sure exactly where it hurt. Her whole arm throbbed with pain. When Bicklo looked up the fighting was over. The three dockers and their wives were staggering across the street towards them. One stumbled and both Bicklo and Snowy ran to help him to his feet.

'You better get the fuck out of here,' Bicklo said. 'The pigs'll be comin'. You really battered the shite out of those Chinks la.' He was proud of the men and he and Snowy almost reverently helped the wounded man into his car. The car moved erratically down Great George Street.

The eight of them hurried up Nelson Street. Snowy and Dee kept a hold on Jean as if it was her ankle that was hurt and not her wrist. They'd reached a hundred yards when Bicklo glanced back.

'Pigs,' he said and slowed down. The others tried to look as casual as he did.

The police car, with a Chinaman sitting next to the driver, slowed down as it passed the kids. The Chinaman studied their faces very carefully and shook his head. The car accelerated and took the corner. They V-signed it when they were sure it was completely out of sight.

Bicklo led them to Upper Pitt Street and hitched himself up on the railings. The others grouped themselves around him. He examined Jean's hand again and shook his head. It was already badly swollen. He touched it and she doubled up and jerked it away. She cradled the wrist gently against her breast.

'It was funny la,' Snowy said. 'The way you screamed "Oh my god."' They all laughed and Jean managed a twitch of her mouth.

'I can't remember what I said,' she said. 'Did I really shout "Oh my god"?' They all said she did and repeated all her actions. Dee was chewing gum and Jean put out her hand like a child. Dee took the gum out and gave it to Jean who chewed it as if it were an anaesthetic. The three girls huddled together to shelter from the cold wind whipping in over the water, while the boys talked about the fight they'd just witnessed.

Marko and Frankie dropped Ato and Robbie off at the Pun Club in Seale Street. The doorway of the club was jammed with black people. They flowed out on to the street and lounged against parked cars. Most of them seemed to have come out for a breath of air, for their faces were shining with sweat. The music wasn't distinct; it just rumbled on the air with a deep bass beat.

Ato could feel his body begin to vibrate in time to the music and he was longing to dive into the deep, dark cave and immerse himself in the blasting black sounds.

'Later la,' he called to Marko. 'Best of luck.'

Marko waved. He didn't need luck. He was smart and this was going to be an easy screw. He calculated, when he split with Frankie, he'd get enough to last him for a long time.

The Pun is a black disco club. It's a small cellar that is always jam-packed with black men and women and white women. Few white men ever enter. Those that do stand uneasily watching the dancers and leave after the first drink. There are half a dozen black clubs in Liverpool which were opened because the other clubs discouraged the black man and refused to play black soul sounds.

Ato began to dance the moment his feet touched the small dance-floor. He danced by himself with his eyes closed. The music had entered his body like some wild spirit that had risen from a grave and had waited centuries to give vent to its energy. He danced fast. His feet jittered, his body shivered like a tuning-fork under a hammer. He twirled and whirled, jumped and split. He was good and it was his own style of dancing. It expressed an inarticulate, crazy joy for life.

Marko settled himself comfortably in the passenger seat and lit a joint. He sucked the smoke and passed the joint to Frankie. Marko felt he was floating on a gentle cushion of air. He was still while the streets and houses and lights zipped by him at high speed.

Briefly the glowing tip of the joint lit up Frankie's face. The shadow of his nose streaked up his forehead. He was much older than Marko and more experienced. He'd just come out after doing three years for robbery with violence. He was a strong, broad-shouldered man who loved wearing very bright colours. At the moment he had on a scarlet shirt with white trousers and a white jacket. He looked cool and knew it. Frankie loved cars and speed. It was his high. The one he was driving was a souped-up Viva filled with gadgetry–stereo tape, radio, rev counter. He drove fast and double-declutched each time he changed gear. The car rocketed and bucked and swayed under his hands. The street-lamps became a fence of blurred lights, the houses endless walls that raced alongside the car, and the road a shiny ribbon that stretched ahead indefinitely. The music and the wind and the drag reduced all their conversation to monosyllables.

Marko felt the world beginning to slow down. Like a twinkling coloured roundabout the houses began to resemble houses as they passed slower and slower. He could recognise their windows and doors and walls. Finally they stopped moving altogether.

'This is it,' Frankie said. He glanced down at a slip of paper in his hand and then up at a house that stood back from the road. It was dark and silent. Frankie studied the house a long time and then glanced up and down the street. The world looked empty. 'It's going to be easy la. That spar of yours said there was no one in, right?'

Marko nodded. The taxi-driver would know. He'd sussed the place out carefully before giving Marko the tip. Marko had told Frankie only because he needed wheels to clean out the house.

'We'll get in round the back, okay,' Frankie said, 'and leave everything to me.' He looked at his watch. 'Give it another five minutes before we move, just to be sure.' He settled back and lit a cigarette. Marko lounged back in imitation. Neither of them saw the man walking up the road towards them.

12

It was one o'clock at last, and Bicklo, Snowy, Paddy and Bill waited on the corner of Great George and St James's Streets. In this way they had a view of both roads and could spot anyone moving towards them. St James's Street stretched out before them like an icy blue shiny serpent encased by street-lamps. It was empty and so was Great George Street. Bicklo patted his hair and undid his shirt another button. Though it was really cold, his shirt was open to the waist. The other three boys shivered and buttoned up. Bicklo ran across the road and looked up St James's towards the city centre. He ran up Great George Street and looked towards the Blackie and beyond. They remained deserted and silent. The four boys looked like the only survivors in an abandoned world.

They waited half an hour and Bicklo never stopped running to peer down the street every five minutes. He was getting impatient, while Snowy and Paddy were feeling the cold bite deep into their bones.

'They're comin',' Bicklo finally shouted. He jumped and danced in the middle of the road. Bill let out a whoop and joined Bicklo. The other two remained shivering where they were.

Two figures, small and indistinct, were moving up St. James's Street towards them. They were too far away, and though Bicklo shielded his eyes and peered he couldn't recognise them.

'Can you see la?' he asked the others. They shook their heads and waited.

Soon two more came into view, and then three and four. Bicklo ran to Great George Street. It was the same. They were coming. He shouted in joy. It was going to be his night; he felt it in his blood. He combed his hair quickly and folded his shirt back so that more of his smooth chest was revealed. The first two figures passed under the street-lamp forty yards away. They were wearing ankle-length dresses and clung to each other. They crossed the road when they saw Bicklo.

Beef! They were coming in droves now. The street was swarming with them in twos and threes or else with their boys. The Cabaret and the other discos had closed and the beef was on its way home. They lived in the tenements along Park Road and further down in the Dingle. This was the quickest route back to their homes and few had the money for cab fares so they walked the long distance back.

Bicklo couldn't control himself any more. He ran to the first two girls.

'You comin' along with us,' he said grinning and nodding to his spars. 'We got a party up in the Yorkie. . . .'

'Fuck off,' one of the beef said. Bicklo laughed. There were so many others just waiting to feel him slide inside their soft, warm pussies. He ran to the next two girls. He knew Sheila; he'd fucked her once. He rapped a while and then ran on.

He and Bill weren't the only ones hustling beef. The streets were suddenly crowded with his spars–ten, fifteen of them– and they were doing the same as Bicklo. It was Saturday night and the beef would be willing. Both the roads were now alive with people–laughing, talking, kissing. The cars flashed by and boys and girls cheered Bicklo on. He waved back and redoubled his efforts. He didn't feel the cold at all. He was covered with shiny sweat as he ran back and forth; rapping the girls, choosing, discarding. God, the whole world was full of beef all dressed up, smelling of perfume, giggling, laughing, holding to each other. And all returning to an empty bed. Bicklo could promise them more. Booze and dry mattresses in a small warm room where they could roll over and over and shout and laugh and moan.

'You comin' along with us,' Bicklo repeated to two new girls. The one he addressed was a sweet-looking pussy. 'We've got a party. . . .'

'It depends,' she said and held his eye.

'C'mon,' Bicklo said and laughed. 'We'll have a great time.' He took her by the arm and gently pulled her. She half-came and half-resisted.

'What do you say, Mary?' she asked her friend. The other girl shrugged and looked pointedly up the road.

'What's your name la?' Bicklo asked. 'I'm Dave. Come on.'

'Cathy,' the girl said and giggled. She nudged her friend. 'We'll see what their party's like and leave if it's awful.'

Bicklo whooped and took Cathy's hand. He ran up towards Nile Street. Cathy tripped and tottered behind him. The other girl walked slowly and reluctantly with Bill, who kept looking desperately at the other beef he was missing out on. He didn't really fancy Mary. She looked a sour pussy.

Marko and Frankie sensed the man standing beside the car. It might have been his faint shadow falling across the bonnet or else the soft rustle of his clothes. They couldn't remember how they knew he was standing by the door, nor for how long he'd been watching them.

'Stay cool,' Frankie whispered. Marko blinked in acknowledgement. They waited it seemed for hours, tense and expectant, before the man made a move. He rapped on the window. Frankie turned his head very slowly and feigned surprise. He jerked his head in a silent question and the man wound his arm round. Frankie, after long thought, did as he was asked and stuck his head out.

'What's up?' he asked.

'You live around here?' the man asked. He bent and peered past Frankie at Marko. It seemed as if he was trying to remember Marko's face.

'We're just resting, man,' Frankie said. 'We're tired and listenin'' to sounds. Anything wrong with that, brother?'

'It just looks suspicious,' he said carefully. 'Why don't you rest somewhere else?'

'Sure,' Frankie said. The man nodded and moved up the road. He looked back at the car and then down at its plate. He was remembering that as well.

Frankie started the car.

'Who's the finger?' Marko asked.

Frankie shrugged and didn't look at Marko. He concentrated very hard. He knew the honky from somewhere; he just couldn't remember from where at the moment. He shoved the car into gear.

'We'd better forget the screw,' he said. 'The bastard has our face and number.'

The headlights lit up the street. The man stood on the corner, glanced at the car and began to cross. Frankie jammed his foot down on the accelerator. Marko fell back in his seat. He could hear the engine roaring, and when he pulled himself up he saw the man jumping back and falling on the pavement. The car rocketed and straightened, the wheels squealed and Frankie changed down and took the corner.

'What you do that for la?' Marko asked in bewilderment. Frankie didn't answer and Marko looked back. A car was coming up very fast and, as he watched, a piercing blue light began to revolve on its roof. Frankie glanced into the driving-mirror and tried to accelerate. His hotted-up machine just didn't have enough speed.

Frankie took the corners faster. The car just couldn't hold the road, it skidded and swayed before he could straighten and by that time the police car was drawing closer. It overtook them just before Smithdown Lane and Frankie cursed. On the big road he knew he could have shaken them off. He slowed down as the police forced him closer and closer to the pavement. He stopped and the police parked diagonally across the street so he'd have had to back to escape.

Marko watched the two pigs get out. They split and came up on either side of the car. He felt cold and slightly ill. He glanced at Frankie. Frankie looked cool; he was lighting a cigarette and Marko thought of doing the same. He didn't have time. The pig opened his door and thumbed him out. Frankie walked slowly round the car, followed by the other pig.

'You nearly knocked a man down there,' the pig said to Frankie.

'He stepped out onto the road just as I was passin' la,' Frankie said. 'I had to swerve to avoid him. Fuck, I nearly crashed myself.'

'You should have stopped, then,' the pig said quietly. 'You may have hurt him.' Frankie shrugged. 'Let's see your papers.'

Frankie handed the pig his driver's licence and car registration. The pig carefully thumbed through the papers and then pocketed them.

'Get in,' he said, and jerked his head to the police car. Frankie began to protest but the pig roughly pushed him to the door. Marko didn't give any trouble. He climbed in and sat quietly. He looked at the passing scenery. They seemed to be returning the way they'd just come. He refused to show any more interest and closed his eyes, and opened them only when the car stopped. The man whom Frankie had nearly run down was standing outside. The pigs made them both get out again and the man studied them and then nodded.

'Those the two,' he announced. 'Bastard nearly got me too.'

'What's all this about,' Frankie asked indignantly. 'He's okay, so let us go.'

'You're going nowhere,' the man said. 'I'm booking you for the attempted murder of a policeman.' He showed his identification.

'You got to be joking,' Frankie said.

The man ignored him and turned to Marko. 'And you as an accomplice. What's your name?'

'Markham,' Marko said softly. 'Ivor Markham.' His voice was as remote as his eyes. He looked as if he was facing his mother once again. The confrontation never seemed to have an end.

Ato watched the fight with clinical interest. He and Robbie were perched on the top step of 116 Upper Stanhope Street. They'd been crossing on their way to the shebeen when a man staggered up the street with a woman on his arm. A second woman was chasing them, shouting and screaming incoherently at the man. He'd stopped and punched her. She fell slowly back like a broken doll, her heels scrabbling on the tarmac as she tried to keep her balance. She only pushed herself further and faster back. Finally she fell flat on her back and her head hit the road so hard that Ato winced. She didn't stay down long. She scrambled up and swung her bag at the man. It caught him on the face and he slammed into a parked car. His white girl-friend waited patiently while he picked himself up and took another swing at the black woman. She went down again and the man took the girl's arm and they hurried into the night. The woman on the street whimpered softly to herself. She stood up swaying and lurched after them.

Ato dusted his trousers. He had a shebeen to attend on Shelborn Street and he was still hungry for music and dance. Robbie and he jogged across Prince's Park Avenue and into Shelborn. They could hear the music faintly. It grew louder as they neared. The street was narrow and like an ancient crone's mouth full of black, rotting gaps where houses had once stood.

'It's goin' to be a hot shebeen la,' Ato said. 'I can feel it.'

The shebeen was being held in a basement. The small room was full of dancing, boozing black people. The noise was deafening, not only of the soul music that boomed from huge speakers but also of laughter and shouting. Ato bought a chilled beer and looked around. It was hot. The men and women were high on liquor and hash, and they were dancing something powerful. Most of the women were hookers, but they weren't here for the money. Tonight they'd give their pussy free for the asking. Ato saw Jonquil and grinned. She was really sexy la, and she enjoyed his body. He

141

slipped through the dancers to her and grabbed her. She laughed and they both moved onto the floor. Though the music was fast, they danced slowly, pressed tightly against each other. Ato could feel the bone of her pelvis, grinding against his. This was going to be a powerful night.

There were five couples lying scattered around on the mattresses. It was so dark, that they could only see each other as blurred, pale outlines. Bicklo was cuddled up with Cathy in a warm corner. He could hear the others whispering and giggling and drinking. They had their own bottle and Bicklo swigged on the whisky and coke and passed it to Cathy. She sipped it and made a face. She took another sip and swallowed. Bicklo slipped his hand into her blouse and his fingers wriggled in under the bra to touch her nipple. She didn't move his hand away and he smiled happily to himself. Her pussy was going to be good.

Snowy could hear the rustling and whispering. He thought of the pussy in Blackpool and sighed. He and Paddy were lying on two mattresses laid in the gym. They shared a bottle of gin and every now and then Snowy would shine the torch around the large, empty hall. Bill had given it to him. The bright beam jerked and slid over the rafters and walls and floor. Snowy could hear other things. He could hear the wind moaning outside and the wooden floor creaking and squeaking. He was sure even the walls were whispering. He sat up and sprayed the light over nearly every inch of the gym. There was nothing. Yet the moment he switched off he could hear the creaks, the groans, the lost, lonely whispers.

'Do you believe in ghosts la,' Snowy asked.

'Yah,' Paddy said shortly. He'd drunk too much and was feeling very sleepy.

'So do I,' Snowy said. 'I mean, it stands to reason there are ghosts la. All those dead people in graveyards.'

Paddy grunted.

'Once when I was running from the pigs, I went to hide in this old building la. It was a big place, sort of like those mansions you see in books. But it was all broken and crumbling la. I was so tired la and I wanted to sleep. I couldn't la. I swear I could hear voices and people moving from room to room. And I heard music too. Not like the music today, sort of funny music la. I got really scared la and I ran.'

Snowy knew he'd seen ghosts that night. They'd risen from the swamp and forgotten graves to haunt this old rich man's house. All they'd found was Snowy and before they could soothe him, tell him who they were–the poor like him–he'd run away. They'd drifted from room to room, searching, but the quarry had long escaped.

'Do you think God made ghosts as well?' Snowy asked.

' 'Course,' Paddy said.

'I mean why doesn't he stop them roamin' around and frightenin' people la,' Snowy demanded. Paddy didn't reply. 'Maybe there's no God la. There's no one at all except us. I mean in the Bible it says God made us la. Right?'

'Yes, that's what it says,' Paddy said very softly. He could feel himself sinking slowly into sleep. He wished Snowy would shut up.

'But then . . . but then . . . in biology class we're taught we came from the apes la. I mean who's right. Either God made us or the apes.'

'I don't know,' Paddy said and added abruptly. 'Goodnight.'

Snowy flashed the torch around the gym once more. He saw nothing. He could hear them in the next room and he could hear other whispers as well. The ghosts were searching again tonight. He wished they'd stop and return to their graves. He wanted to think. In school they taught you one thing, in church another. People told you that you could have everything you saw on the telly; then when you took it they punished you. They sent men to the moon but they never had enough money to give him. There were so many things Snowy couldn't understand in the world. He wanted to go on thinking, but he was beginning to feel sleepy. People would say one thing, then they said another. He was baffled and came to a single conclusion.

'They really fuck your mind up,' he announced to Paddy. There was no reply. Paddy was fast asleep. Snowy huddled closer to Paddy and curled himself up into a ball to keep out the cold. He held tightly to the torch in case the ancient spirits came too close.